PRAISE FOR
JAMES HOUSTON'S INUI'

TIKTALIKTAK

"A short story, economically written, with the sharp realism of an actual, stark adventure . . . a true hero tale, distinctively and forcefully illustrated."—*The Horn Book*

"A grim and moving saga of human courage and the harsh means of survival."—*Library Journal*

THE WHITE ARCHER

"[Told] with dramatic and moving fervor . . . a mighty legend and a proud one."—*Publishers Weekly*

"The vivid, moving story of [Kanguq's] triumph over hatred . . . reflects James Houston's knowledge and appreciation of Eskimo character and culture."—*Booklist*

"There is an epic quality to this short book . . . In this rugged tale . . . the reader sees a primitive yet dignified and poetic civilization."—*The New York Times Book Review*

- JAMES HOUSTON'S -
TREASURY
OF INUIT
LEGENDS

- JAMES HOUSTON'S -

TREASURY
OF INUIT
LEGENDS

◆◆◆◆◆◆◆◆◆◆◆◆◆◆◆◆◆◆◆

AN ODYSSEY / HARCOURT YOUNG CLASSIC

HARCOURT, INC.

Orlando   Austin   New York   San Diego   Toronto   London

www.HarcourtBooks.com

Stories copyright © 1965 (Tiktaliktak), 1967 (The White Archer),
1968 (Akavak), and 1971 (Wolf Run) by James Houston

First Odyssey/Harcourt Young Classics editions 2006

Library of Congress Cataloging-in-Publication Data
Houston, James A., 1921–2005
[Selections. 2006]
James Houston's Treasury of Inuit legends/James Houston.
p.   cm.
"Odyssey/Harcourt Young Classic."
1. Inuit—Folklore.   2. Inuit mythology.   3. Tales—North America.
4. Legends—North America.   I. Title.   II. Title: Treasury of Inuit legends.
E99.E7H858   2006
398.2089'9712—dc22   2006043577
ISBN-13: 978-0-15-205924-8   ISBN-10: 0-15-205924-5
ISBN-13: 978-0-15-205930-9 pb   ISBN-10: 0-15-205930-X pb

Text set in AGaramond
Designed by Scott Piehl

First edition
H G F E D C B A   H G F E D C B A (pb)

Printed in the United States of America

Although we will meet no more in this world,
we look forward to reuniting in that happy place.
Jamasie—Saumik—we are forever thankful to you,
as you left with us, the people of Cape Dorset,
the ability to make our living. We will always
remember our close fellowship.

> —Kananginak Pootoogook,
>   artist and printmaker, Cape Dorset,
>   Nunavut Territory, 2005

· CONTENTS ·

· ABOUT JAMES HOUSTON ·

by Theodore Taylor

I first learned about Canadian writer and artist James Houston from Mrs. Ida Kapakatoak, an Inuk of the Hunters and Trappers Organization of Kugluktuk, Nunavut, the new Canadian polar territory. Ida said Houston was the greatest Arctic voice who had ever lived. She was totally correct.

I'd hired her to teach me how to skin a seal, necessary for research on my own book, *Ice Drift,* a novel about two young Inuit brothers and their husky sled dog who drift almost eighteen hundred miles down the Greenland Strait on an ice floe, sometimes facing hungry polar bears, other times blizzards. They'd been seal hunting when the ice attached to the shore was hit by a berg and broke away. Researching the story was my introduction to the Inuit culture. Ida taught me by phone and mailed drawings and diagrams.

I'd planned a flight to Churchill, on the Hudson Bay, to observe the migration of the polar bears down to the ice to hunt seal and walrus. But my cardiologist said, "No! If you have another heart attack there you may not be able to be flown out." I almost wept.

So instead, I began teaching myself about the Arctic by taking Ida's advice and reading Houston. His memoir, *Confessions of an Igloo Dweller: The Story of the Man Who Brought Inuit Art to the Outside World,* was a gold mine. In it, Houston told of the first time he encountered the Arctic, in 1948. He joined a friend who had a pontoon aircraft on a mission to save the life of a baby chewed up by sled dogs. A doctor accompanied them on the life-or-death flight. Houston brought along his sleeping bag, warm clothes, and his sketch pad. He was already an artist. Photos of him in those early days show a face of intellect and great strength.

The seaplane landed deep in the Arctic near Canso Bay and the doctor was carried ashore on a hunter's back. Meanwhile, Houston was sketching the Inuit of the tent village.

The doctor came back in three minutes with the baby in arms and yelled to Houston that they'd take off immediately for several stages of flight to Montreal and the Royal Victoria Hospital.

James declared he wasn't going. (The baby survived, he heard months later.) He was staying in the Arctic. After a few trips south, one to get married, he would end up living among the Inuit for the next fourteen years.

No writer I've ever read about had the determination and guts displayed by Houston, putting himself in native hands, unable to speak a single word of their language, Inuktitut, having never eaten raw seal, raw walrus, or raw fish. He used his sketching to help learn their language. He became a student of whom they were proud. The Inuit affectionately named him Saumik: "the left-handed one."

James Archibald Houston was born June 12, 1921, in Toronto, his father an adventuresome clothing importer, mother solidly artistic, bent on James going in that direction. James and his younger sister would crawl into bed with their parents and listen to their father tell stories of Sioux Indians.

When he was eight or nine, James caught scarlet fever and his mother brought him a book that was entirely blank. She said, "If you want a book, make one yourself." He did, writing and illustrating a story about a shipwrecked boy. When he was twelve, he began attending classes at the Toronto Art Gallery, and continued to do so for the next four years. Serving in the Toronto Scottish Regiment for five years during World War II, finishing as a warrant officer, he kept up his self-education as an artist, drawing fellow soldiers. There was further art education in Paris, and later in Japan.

Houston could look back on his time with the Inuit of the Arctic as the most creative in his career. Those fourteen years of hunting and eating their food, wearing their style of clothing, tending his own team of dogs, riding on and running beside their sleds gave him experiences rarely granted to a *Qallunaaq* (pronounced "kabloona"), a white person.

He learned about *tuvag*—ice—and snow from them. He learned about *nanuit*—polar bears—and killed several. He learned about sitting above a seal hole with a harpoon; learned about the birds— the dovekies, the ravens, the gyrfalcons, the ptarmigans, the geese, and the snowy owls. He learned about the mock moons in the summer when the moon resembled pale white cheese, when wolves got to herds of musk oxen before the Inuit hunters did. In February, he watched the aurora borealis streamers in twilight as they moved from west to east, forming a curtain of yellow and white. He saw floe ice cover all the bays, inlets, and straits during the winters, usually strong enough to carry sleds, dog teams, and humans. Inuit elders taught him about *Nanurluk,* the polar bear spirit; about *Nuliajuk,* the goddess of the sea; about *uqalurait,* the snowdrift spirits; and *tuurngait,* powerful spirits for good or evil.

Inuit women in the camps and settlements sewed him parkas of caribou or seal for the colder weather and trade cloth for the summer. Shoes, *kamiks,* were made of sealskin; his feet were kept warm and dry by wearing many layers of socks made of animal skins. The dog sleds, *qamutiik,* were made of wooden planks with steel runners, which were covered in a thick layer of mud and then iced.

It was this life that James Houston celebrated, even worshipped—all of it.

In 1955, at the request of the Canadian government, James Houston became the first civil administrator of West Baffin Island and traveled the 65,000-square-mile territory by dog sled, camping with the Inuit population, learning how they told their stories. He knew all of these things before he wrote and illustrated the first of his seventeen books for children and fourteen for adults, providing illustrations for most of them. He also illustrated nine more books by other authors.

Additionally, Houston produced and directed many documentary films, and he wrote and co-produced the feature film *The White Dawn* for Paramount Pictures in 1973. He also worked as master designer for Steuben Glass. Among his many contributions to global art was his campaign to promote carvings of the Inuit. The Canadian Handicrafts Guild, now the Canadian Guild of Crafts, assisted in the marketing of what is now internationally recognized as Inuit art. Houston has been credited with the introduction of contemporary Inuit art to the world. His awards are numerous, including Canada's highest honor, Officer of the Order of Canada; three Book of the Year for Children Awards from the Canadian Library Association; and several honorary college degrees.

Of his own work, Houston wrote, "To hold attention of one's readers, I believe an author should try to tell a story that possesses truth, interesting characters, and is enhanced by an unusual environment. It should possess, as well, a driving sense of purpose and excitement." James Houston achieved all of these things in his stunning performance as both a writer and an artist.

When James Houston died in the spring of 2005, he left behind enduring works about the Arctic and Inuit. He also survives in the hearts of the Inuit and other aboriginal peoples, his family and friends, and his readers of all ages.

- JAMES HOUSTON'S -

TREASURY
OF INUIT
LEGENDS

TIKTALIKTAK

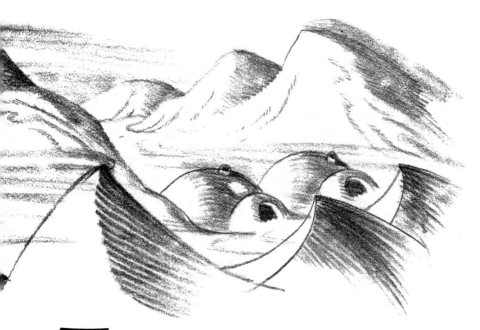

Tiktaliktak drove his long, sharp chisel into a crack and pulled himself up to the top of the jagged ice. From this height, he looked east and west along the rough barrier ice forced against the coastline as far as he could see.

He looked back along his trail of footprints across the snow-covered shore to his father's igloo, now almost hidden by the three hills that protected it from the howling winds that rushed over their island.

Tiktaliktak's people were sea hunters, singers, carvers, builders of sleek kayaks, masters of swift dog teams, whale hunters, listeners at the breathing places in the ice.

Because his father had always been a clever hunter, Tiktaliktak had grown up knowing only good times in the house of his family. There had always been great sea beasts for feasting, fat red trout, snow geese, and sometimes meat from the swift herds of caribou that roved beyond the mountains on the inland plain.

There had also been singing and laughter in the house of his father, and hunters from distant camps had come to visit, bringing with them their whole families.

But at the end of this winter, the animals had fled from the plain. The birds had not yet returned from the south, and the fish remained locked beneath the frozen lakes.

The wind had blown in the wrong direction during the moons of February and March, holding masses of loose ice against the shores so that no man could travel or hunt on the sea. It was a time for starving.

Tiktaliktak thought of his family lying in the dark snowhouse without food for themselves or seal oil for their lamps. Hunger stirred within him. He knew he must find a way to help them.

The young Inuk climbed carefully down from his high place on the ice through the great pieces that surrounded him like sharp white teeth. The sea ice that lay before him had been broken many times. It had opened and closed and frozen again until he did not know where to place his feet for fear of falling through. In some places, the ice was much thicker than the height of a man; in other spots, it was thinner than his little finger. A light layer of new snow covered everything, hiding the danger from his eyes.

Before each step, Tiktaliktak felt the ice in front of him with the chisel on the end of his harpoon. Many times the sharp point broke through the thin surface and water flooded over the snow at his feet. He was forced to try one way and then another before finding ice strong enough to hold his weight. He moved forward cautiously, so that it took a long time to travel even a short distance.

Tiktaliktak was lean and strong for his age, with a handsome tanned face, wide cheekbones, and a fine hawklike nose. Like all the people of his race, he possessed quick dark eyes with the lids drawn narrow for protection against long winters on the treeless plain, where they hunted in the wind and sun and snow. He wore narrow-slitted sun goggles.

His square white teeth flashed when he smiled, and his jaw muscles, strong from eating meat, showed clearly. His hair hung straight and black almost to his shoulders. It glistened in the cold morning sunlight like the bright new wings of an Arctic butterfly, and the butterfly was Tiktaliktak's namesake.

Tiktaliktak wished most of all to be a good hunter. He could already throw a harpoon with great skill and drive an arrow straight to its mark. He thrilled at the songs and chanting and the great whirling and drumming of the hunters as they performed the autumn and midwinter dances before the hunt.

But the magic of the dancers, and all their hunts, had failed them this year.

As he moved slowly forward testing the ice, Tiktaliktak saw before him the trail made by a huge white bear. Each of its paws had left a mark in the snow as large as if a man had sat down. Looking closely, Tiktaliktak could see that the tracks were fresh and new, for the print of each pad was still sharp and clear.

The bear must have been hungry, too, for its track led away from the land, which meant it had been forced to make the long crossing in search of new hunting grounds. Tiktaliktak hoped that the bear had not seen him, for he did not wish to fight on this thin ice. Farther along, he could see where the bear's immense weight had broken through the ice, but this meant nothing to the huge beast with its thick waterproof fur. It had crawled out of the freezing water and continued on its way.

Tiktaliktak traveled until late afternoon. Ahead of him lay the dark stretch of sea water beyond the ice. Half hidden in the winter fog above the water flew thousands of seabirds in thick black flocks. They gave the young hunter new strength, for he knew that there must also be seals in the dark water, and the birds and seals would provide food and oil for the lamps of his people.

Small icebergs caught and frozen fast towered above his head, offering him shelter in their weird shadowy blue caves. In the haze beyond them, water and ice and sky seemed to blend into one. The pale orange sun was surrounded by a great circle of light. In this circle appeared four false suns and beyond them four more. These reflections, called sun dogs, were seldom seen, and Tiktaliktak knew they were a warning of storms to come. His people believed them to be the team of dogs pulling the sun on its endless journey through the sky.

When Tiktaliktak reached the edge of the sea ice, he saw many flocks of birds upon the water. Excitedly, he began to plan the hunt. He would hide downwind of the birds, behind a large piece of up-turned ice near the water's edge. The rafts of birds would drift near

enough for his arrows to reach them, and when hit, the birds would float in to him.

Nearer and nearer drifted the birds, in countless screaming numbers. Tiktaliktak's arrows flew straight, and the birds they hit floated in as he had hoped, all save one small seabird that floated past the point where he was hiding and was blown by the wind to the far edge of the ice.

When his last arrow was gone, Tiktaliktak stood up. A few birds took off in panic, and then the others followed in great flights. They flew down the coast beyond his sight.

Tiktaliktak picked the soft warm feathered birds out of the water, and after recovering his arrows, he piled them on the ice and

started out after the small bird that had drifted beyond him. With much difficulty, he finally reached it with his harpoon and pulled it to the edge of the ice. When he turned to retrace his steps to the pile of birds, a huge crack had opened in the ice, barring his path. It was too wide to jump. Tiktaliktak realized with horror that he could not return. He was drifting out to sea on a large pan of ice, carried by the rising wind and tide.

It was growing colder and soon would be dark. Tiktaliktak squatted on the ice and ate the small seabird, thinking of the precious pile of food only a short distance away. He would never see it again, nor perhaps his home.

He felt somewhat better after eating the bird and with his short

knife tried to pry loose some ice to build a small snowhouse. But all he could manage was to stand some flat pieces upright, leaning them together like a tent. The cracks between the ice he filled with snow to complete a rough protection against the night wind. Curled up in this tiny shelter, he dared not sleep for fear of freezing.

All through the night, the small ice island moved with the tide. It sighed and groaned, and he wondered if it would break apart and cast him into the freezing sea.

When dawn came, he walked around his tiny frozen island, waving his arms to warm himself. He wondered about his family and what they must be thinking.

The open water around his moving ice floe sent moisture into the freezing air. It rose as a dark fog against the pale light of morning and fell back into the leaden sea, covering his ice floe with countless frost crystals that turned it into a silent, shimmering magic place.

Suddenly, a seal's dark head came up through the water close to the edge of the ice. Tiktaliktak was ready with his harpoon, but the seal was frightened at finding itself so near a human and quickly ducked beneath the surface before the sharp point could reach him. To bring the seal back, Tiktaliktak began to call the words *"Qaigit, qaigit, qaigit"* (Come, come, come). Then he lay on the edge of the ice floe and, with the end of his knife, reached over and gently scratched just below the surface of the freezing water, imitating the sound of a seal's front claws opening a breathing hole in the ice. This sound often makes a curious seal come near. But not this one, nor did any other appear, though Tiktaliktak continued with magic words and scratching until well past midday.

In the afternoon, he walked around his small floating ice island, trying to keep warm, until a new cold wind came out of the northeast, chilling his very bones and changing the direction of his drifting home.

He improved his icehouse as much as he could and spread fresh snow on the floor to serve as a bed, for he would be warmer lying on snow than on ice. Before he lay down, he put one of his sealskin mitts beneath his hip and the other beneath his shoulder.

That night, Tiktaliktak drew his arms inside his fur parka, hugging them close to his body so they would not freeze, and he breathed into his hood to help warm himself. In this way, he managed to sleep, dreaming all night of eating rich haunches of caribou, fat young loons, and the sweet summer eggs of snow geese.

As the first light of dawn crept around his tiny house, Tiktaliktak felt a gentle bump and then another. Rising quickly, he went outside the ice shelter.

His island had drifted against another much larger ice pan. Gathering his precious harpoon, bow and arrows, and his short knife, he ran lightly to the edge of the ice. First he tested the strength of the larger pan with the end of his harpoon; then he leaped across the narrow opening just as the two pieces began to draw apart.

This second drifting island felt much stronger as he walked carefully over it, feeling beneath the snow covering with his ice chisel. It did not have as many cracks or thin dangerous places as the first pan.

Through the narrow slits of his snow goggles, Tiktaliktak saw something dark spread out on the snow before him. As he hurried toward it, a huge black raven rose up and flew away. The dark stain was a patch of blood on the snow where, as the tracks leading up to it showed, a white bear had killed a seal. But, alas, the bear and almost all the seal meat were gone. Only one small fatty scrap remained, for the hungry raven had carefully cleaned away everything else left by the bear.

Nearby, Tiktaliktak found some large flat pieces of ice and started to build a new shelter. He soon tired because he was so hungry, but he continued to work until his house was completed. Then

he placed the scrap of meat beside a small hole in the roof and
crawled inside to wait.

Before long, he heard the swish of wings as the raven returned.
The sleek black bird landed on the spot where the seal had been
and, finding nothing, rose up with an angry croak. It landed again,
this time on top of Tiktaliktak's house, ready to snatch the last remaining morsel of seal fat.

In an instant, Tiktaliktak's hand shot up through the hole,
grasped the raven's leg, and pulled it down into the house. Some say

ravens are not good to eat; they are wrong. The raven was thin but delicious, and Tiktaliktak felt much better after this fine breakfast.

For three days and three nights, he walked about on his floe to warm himself and slept when he could. The winds and strong tides moved his island back and forth, sometimes out to sea, sometimes toward the land. He found nothing more to eat and felt he would surely die on this lonely ice island.

On the fourth day, Tiktaliktak awoke and sensed that something had changed. He looked out of his house, and there before him was the most welcome sight he had ever seen. In the distance, like a gigantic stony cloud, lay the island called Sakkiak, its raw granite hills piercing through the surrounding shore ice. These hills were swept entirely free of snow by the wind. Tiktaliktak knew that no man dared to live on Sakkiak, but it was solid rock, and he longed to leave his ice island and place his foot upon it, though it was a bleak and lonely place.

He judged the drift of his ice pan with great care and saw that he would come close to the shore ice surrounding the large island. He realized, too, that his ice floe might not touch it and might be swept forever out into the open sea.

Tiktaliktak planned now to try a desperate trick he had once heard of. If it failed, he would surely die.

He ran to the thinnest corner of his floating island where he had noticed a piece of ice that had cracked off and then partly refrozen. It was not much larger than a walrus, but if he could break it loose, it might keep him afloat and serve as a clumsy boat. He worked frantically with his chisel, trying to free the corner as he

drew nearer and nearer to the long floe of loose ice stretching out from the island. He could see now that he would pass the long floe without touching.

Suddenly, the small piece of ice broke beneath his chisel and was free. With a quick jump, he landed upon it and, kneeling down, paddled desperately with his hands in the freezing water. The ice boat was moving, and in a short time he touched against the loose ice that stretched in a wide broken path to the island.

Now came the most daring part of the trick. Arranging his bow and arrow quiver so they hung straight down his back and holding his harpoon with both hands before him at the level of his chest to steady his balance, Tiktaliktak started running and jumping from pan to pan with every bit of skill he possessed.

If he dared to stop even for a moment, the small pieces of ice would roll or sink in the icy water and he would fall. He moved with the balance and delicacy of a sandpiper skirting a wave on a beach until he made a final leap onto the strong shore ice surrounding the island. There he lay, gasping.

As his breath returned to him, Tiktaliktak could scarcely believe that he had reached solid ice and was still alive. Slowly he walked toward the sheltering hills of the great barren island that rose before him, grateful to be on land once more.

He chose a valley that formed a long sheltered passage leading upward to the top of the island. In this valley, under the protecting hills, he built a small strong snowhouse and slept he knew not how long. After this, he lost all track of time.

Tiktaliktak awoke with raging pangs of hunger and hurried out to see what treasures his new island might provide. Weak as he was from lack of food, it took a full day to walk the length of the island. Although Sakkiak was fairly narrow, it also took him a day to cross it because of the steep rocky spine of hills that ran its whole length.

The beaches were blown almost clear. Snow had been driven against the hills in hard wind-packed drifts many times the height of a man. Tiktaliktak walked along the frozen beaches, searching them for any kind of food and peering out hopefully over the shore ice for seals.

Nothing did he see but snow and rock and sometimes bleached white bones or hard dry scraps of bird skins eaten out a season

before by foxes. The lemmings, small rodents without tails, seemed not to be on the island, for he saw no tracks. The fat eider ducks had left evidence everywhere, in the form of old nesting places, of their summer occupation of the island. But by the time they returned to lay their eggs, he would surely be dead of hunger.

Often he gazed out across the straits, where the white ice floes churned past in the dangerous rip tides. He could see the mainland hanging blue and serene like a dream of some far-off place. There was his home, his family, his friends. All of them must think that he was dead. The mainland seemed near, and yet to Tiktaliktak, without food or materials or a boat, it was an impossible distance.

Staggering from hunger and fatigue, he returned to the snow-house that evening and had terrible dreams until he awoke in the morning in the cold gray igloo scarcely knowing whether he was truly awake or still in some dark nightmare.

When he climbed the hill the next day, Tiktaliktak used his harpoon for support, like an old man. He had to tell himself again and again that he had lived fewer than twenty summers.

From the top of the rocky hill, Tiktaliktak saw far out on the drifting ice many walrus, fat, sleek, and brown, lying together motionless like great stones, their tusks showing white in the sunlight. The wind was carrying them away, out to sea, and he could never hope to take one.

Sitting there in the cold wind, with no help, he said aloud, over and over again, "This island is my grave. This island is my grave. I shall never leave this place. I shall never leave this place." The idea obsessed him, and at last, in fright, he hurriedly stumbled downward, falling many times, until he came to the snowhouse and slept again for a very long while.

When he awoke, Tiktaliktak cut small strips from the tops of his boots and chewed them to ease his hunger. This seemed to give him some strength. Then, slowly, as if drawn by magic, he started again up the long hill.

It was warmer now. True spring was coming to the land. But it helped him not at all, for there was nothing living on the island, nor would there be until the birds came to nest again, and that would be too late for him.

On top of the hill once more, Tiktaliktak scanned the sea and saw nothing but water and glaring ice. Again a distant voice seemed to say, "This island is your grave." He stood up slowly and looked around. There were many great flat rocks, and Tiktaliktak decided they would be his final resting place. Two of the largest ones lay near each other, offering him a sheltered bed, and with his failing strength, he dragged two more large stones to make the ends, at head and foot. Another large one placed on top covered the lower half. The stones now formed a rough coffin.

He searched until he found a large flat piece to cover his head. Half laughing and half crying, he climbed into his stony grave. After one last look at the wide blue sky and the sea around him, he lay down with his harpoon, knife, and bow arranged neatly by his side. He hoped that his relatives would someday find his bones and know him by his weapons and know what had happened to him.

Tiktaliktak did not know how long he slept. When he awoke, he was numb with cold. Slowly, a new idea started to form in his mind: "I will not die, I will not die, I will not die." With a great effort, he pushed away the stone that formed the top half of the coffin. Painfully, he arose and staggered out of that self-made grave.

Holding himself as straight as he could with the aid of his harpoon, Tiktaliktak staggered down the side of the hill to the beach. He lay there to rest and again fell asleep. This time he dreamed of many strange things: skin boats rising up from their moorings, haunches of fat year-old caribou, rich dark walrus meat, young ducks with delicious yellow fat, juicy seals, and the warm eggs of a snow owl.

He could not tell if he was asleep or awake, but again and again the head of a seal appeared. It seemed so real in the dream that he took up his harpoon and cast it blindly before him. He felt a great jerk that fully awakened him, and, behold, he had a true seal firmly harpooned. He lay back with his feet against a rock and held on to the harpoon line until the seal's spirit left him.

With his last strength, Tiktaliktak drew the seal out of the water and across the edge of the ice until he had all this richness in his hands. He knew that the seal had been sent to him by the sea spirit and that this gift would give him back his life.

After some food and sleep, and more food and sleep again, he soon felt well. Using his bow, he whirled an arrow swiftly into a hollow scrap of driftwood and dried shavings until they grew hot, smoked, and burst into flames. The seal fat burned nicely in a hollow stone in his snowhouse, making it warm and bright. The spring

sun helped to restore his health and strength, and Tiktaliktak remembered once more that he was young.

He kept the meat of the seal in the igloo and prepared the fat for use in the stone lamp. The sealskin he turned inside out without splitting it open and scraped it with a flattened bone in the special way that he had seen his mother teach his sister.

One day, he found the tracks of a white fox that had come to the island. After that, the fox came to visit his dwelling every day. It always came along the same way, and that was its mistake.

Tiktaliktak built a falling-stone trap across its path, baited with a scrap of seal meat.

The next morning, the fox was in the trap, and after skinning it, Tiktaliktak drew from the tail long strong sinews that make the finest thread. That evening he ate the fox meat and placed the fine white skin above his oil lamp to dry. Tiktaliktak also made a good needle by sharpening a thin splinter of bone on a rock, and with this, he mended his clothes.

After his work was done, he stepped out through the entrance of the small igloo to look at the great night sky. It was filled with stars beyond counting that formed patterns familiar to all his people, who used them for guidance when traveling.

Off to the north, great green and yellow lights soared up, slowly faded, then soared again in their magic way. Tiktaliktak's people knew that these were caused by the night spirits playing the kicking game in the sky. In the way his father had taught him, he whistled and pushed his hands up to the sky, marveling as the lights ebbed and flowed with his movements as though he controlled them.

Life on the island was better now, but still Tiktaliktak longed to return home to his own people.

Half of another moon passed, and now the spring sun hung just below the horizon each night and would not let the sky grow dark. Two seals appeared in the open waters of the bay in front of the snowhouse, and by good fortune, Tiktaliktak managed to harpoon first one and then the other. This gave him an abundance of food and of oil to heat his igloo. He again carefully drew the meat out of the seals, without cutting them open in the usual method, and scraped and dried the skins.

Tiktaliktak sat before his small house thinking and making plans. An idea for building a kind of boat without any tools or driftwood for the frame had finally come to him.

He began to prepare one of the three sealskins. First, he tied the skin tightly and carefully where the back flippers had been so that no water could enter. Then where the seal's neck had been, he bound in a piece of bone, hollow through the middle. When he had finished, he put his mouth to the hole and, with many strong breaths, blew the skin up so that it looked again like a fat seal. Next, he fitted a small piece of driftwood in the bone to act as a plug and hold in the air.

The sun was warm on his back as he worked with his floats on that bright spring morning. His stomach was full, his clothes were mended, and he began to make a song inside himself, hoping that someday he might return to his people on the mainland. The song had magic in it. It spoke of fear and wonder and of life and hope. The words came well. There was joy in Tiktaliktak and yet a warning of danger, too.

He looked up from his work as a huge shadow loomed over him. Tiktaliktak threw himself sideways, rolling toward his harpoon, which he caught hold of as he sprang to his feet. Before him, between his small house and the sea, stood a huge white bear. The bear's mouth was half open, and its blue-black tongue lolled between its strong teeth. Its little eyes were watching him warily as it decided how best to kill him.

Fear stirred the hair on the back of Tiktaliktak's neck and reached down into his stomach. His harpoon was small for a beast

such as this one, and although he had often heard of encounters with bears, Tiktaliktak had never met one face to face.

Remembering the wise words of his father, Tiktaliktak carefully studied every movement of the bear. He tried to think like a bear to understand what the great beast would do next. He slowly knelt down and felt with the chisel end of the harpoon for a crack between two rocks. Finding this, he wedged it in firmly and leveled the pointed end at the bear's throat. He had not long to wait for the attack.

The bear lunged forward, and the harpoon pierced the white fur and went deep into its throat. Tiktaliktak held the harpoon as long as he could, then rolled away, but not before he felt the bear's great claws rake the side of his face. He scrambled to his feet and ran uphill.

The huge beast tried to follow, but the harpoon caught and caught again in the rocks, forcing the point more deeply inward. The harpoon found its life, and with a great sigh, the bear's spirit rushed out and it was dead.

Tiktaliktak's face was numb at first. Then it started to throb with pain. He made his way slowly to a small hillside stream that flowed from the melting snow down to the sea. There he washed his face in the clear icy water.

Returning to his snowhouse, he took a patch of foxskin the size of his hand, scraped and scrubbed it clean, and set it squarely over the terrible wound. As it dried, the clean patch of foxskin tightened and grew smaller. It drew the open wounds together, almost forming a new skin on his face.

Tiktaliktak was weak after his fight with the bear and nervous of every shadow. Also, he feared that his wound might fester, so he washed the foxskin dressing often. In time, his face showed signs of healing, and the pain ceased to bother him.

Then Tiktaliktak set about making a little stone and sod house for the summer like the ancient houses of his forefathers. He had no material to make the kind of sealskin tent now used by his people.

Inside the new house, it was warm and comfortable, and the light from his small lamp glowed brightly. The new bearskin was warm to sleep on and the meat good to eat. At this time, another

seal came to him one evening in the half dark of spring before the moon had fully risen. It did not see Tiktaliktak until his harpoon reached it.

Cutting this seal open in the usual way, from the rear flippers to the throat, Tiktaliktak then scraped and stretched the skin. With the skin, he made new hip-length boot tops to sew above his own. These, bound with drawstrings and packed with dried moss, were quite waterproof.

He had placed the two shoulder blades of the white bear under a stone in the water so that the sea lice would pick them clean as snow. He now bound them firmly with seal thongs to each end of his harpoon. In this way, he made a strong double-bladed paddle.

On a windless day, he tied the three blown-up sealskins together and placed them in the shallow water. Sitting astride them, he balanced himself and floated. It took some practice before he was able to hold steady and paddle and control this strange craft, but a boat of any kind seemed his only chance of reaching the mainland again.

By day, Tiktaliktak would look out over the great expanse of water with its treacherous tides and wonder if he had lived through this terrible spring only to drown. At night, he would dream of his mother, his father, and his sisters. He wondered if they had starved or had found food as he had and were still alive.

He must try to make the crossing. First, he gathered a small parcel of meat, which he wrapped in seal fat so it would float and covered with sealskin so that it would be protected from the salt of the sea. Tiktaliktak tied the package to his waist with a thong, and it floated nicely behind him like a small duck. He filled two seal bladder pouches with fresh water, and these he hung around his neck.

The next morning was gray with fog, but the wind was down, and he decided this would be the day to start the dangerous journey. Pushing the inflated sealskin floats into the water, Tiktaliktak carefully climbed onto the strange watercraft. Then he started out, with only one glance back at his island home and upward to his open grave on top of the hill.

Cautiously, he began to use the bone paddle to steer out into the current, which swirled away from the island and carried him into the open water of the strait. With alarm, he noticed the great strength of the tide as it swept him eastward instead of north to the mainland as he had hoped. Tiktaliktak paddled very gently, careful not to upset his frail craft, learning as he went to guide it with his feet, which hung down awkwardly like those of a young snow goose trying to swim for the first time.

Tiktaliktak tried not to look down, for he could see far below him in the clear gray water great fronds of seaweed waving mysteriously, moved by powerful underwater currents. A light breeze rippled over the surface of the water, sending him out toward the center of the strait. He could see the riptides now pressing down or swelling upward in a smooth icy rush. His feet and legs began to feel the freezing grip of the water, although they stayed dry. The chill of the sea drove through his boots, moss packing, and heavy fur socks, leaving him numb with cold.

Slowly, the hills of Sakkiak grew smaller and turned blue in the distance. Tiktaliktak judged himself to be halfway to the mainland. He paddled gently to give himself direction in the fast-moving current and was carried on the tide through gray patches of mist that hung over the water. Now stiff with cold and thirsty, he managed to drink a little of the fresh water from one of the pouches that hung around his neck, and paddled on through the eerie silence.

Suddenly, Tiktaliktak heard a familiar sound, a sound he feared. It boomed across the water again and again, the great grunting roar of a huge bull walrus. The tide was carrying him straight into the herd the walrus was jealously protecting.

Dark heads appeared as the large herd grouped together, peering weak-eyed at this new intruder. Almost all of them showed the long thin tusks of female walrus.

The old bull separated from the herd, ready for combat. It started to rear up in the water, trying to see and also to frighten the new enemy, while working itself into a fury. Tiktaliktak knew that to the

poor eyesight of the beast he would look like another walrus trying to enter the herd.

With a roaring bellow, the great bull, flashing its white tusks, dove beneath the surface and went straight at Tiktaliktak. He braced himself, expecting to be lifted from the water, when to his surprise the old bull rose up before him locked in combat with a powerful young male walrus.

Tiktaliktak watched them struggle, their tusks ripping and locking, their eyes rolling. The water around them frothed white and then turned red with blood.

By good fortune, helped by the tide and steady paddling, Tiktaliktak was carried safely away. The huge struggling beasts thrashed in the sea, never noticing that he had drifted onward.

Seabirds screamed around him, and he felt the welcome pull of the tide as it drew him at last toward the shores of the mainland.

The dark granite cliffs seemed to tower over him when he drifted into their shadows. Delicate lacings of snow on the cliffs glowed in the long rays of the evening sun.

Suddenly, with a bump that almost upset him, Tiktaliktak felt solid rock beneath his feet. He stumbled ashore, scarcely able to stand on his numb, nearly frozen legs. Looking back over the waters he had crossed, he was filled with gratitude that the spirits who guard the land and sea and sky had allowed him to make his dangerous journey.

Dragging behind him the three inflated sealskins, Tiktaliktak struggled over the rocky beach while the first shower of summer rain beat against his face. With his knife, he cut the thongs that held the bone paddle blades to his harpoon, and it again became his weapon. He then cut the three skin floats open from end to end, and placing the dry inside of one beneath himself, he stretched the other two over himself and fell deeply asleep.

He was awakened by the damp cold the next morning. The mists of early summer hung down everywhere, obscuring the cliffs and the seabirds that cried above him.

Joyful at the thought of being once again on the mainland after so many moons, he jumped up, ate some of the meat in his small package, drank some fresh water from a nearby stream, and set out along the coast toward the west. Although Tiktaliktak had never traveled in this part of the country before, he knew it would be easier and safer to stay on the coast than to risk a straighter path across the mountains. Climbing would use up his strength, and perhaps he would lose his way.

Tiktaliktak walked for two long days and slept at night under rock ledges like a wild animal. Then he came to a narrow inlet that he had never seen before, but he recognized it from his grandfather's description as the bay called The Place of Beautiful Stones.

Walking fearfully along the edge of the small half-hidden cove, it did indeed seem like a place from another world. The gray rock cliffs that stood above him had the weird forms of ancient giants. At the end of the small bay, a well-worn path led up to the mouth of a dark cave in the crumbling rock wall.

Tiktaliktak stood before it in the gloom of the late afternoon listening for some sound, almost afraid to enter, yet eager to see for himself the inside of this strange place.

Hearing nothing save the dripping of water, he bent down and stepped quickly into the cave. Its entrance was small, but the cave was large inside and rose to a great height. When his eyes grew accustomed to the half darkness, he knelt down and examined the floor of the cave.

It was covered with smooth round white pebbles, and among them lay a number of shining red stones. These were so sharply cut that Tiktaliktak's people believed they could only have been shaped by strange men or spirits. There were also other stones cut in this wondrous way, and as clear as water, they glowed like the waning moon even in the half darkness.

Tiktaliktak looked to the wall on his left, and there, just as his grandfather had said, were two neat rows of holes, exactly as many as he had fingers and toes, each containing a fox skull bleached

white with age. Near these, embedded in the walls, were more red stones that seemed to wink like eyes in the fading light.

Some said that this was an ancient secret place of the little people who used to rule the land. It was here they came to collect and cut the precious stones they loved to have and to trade sometimes with other people.

Tiktaliktak gathered a few stones and would have taken more, but he heard a tapping sound deep in the cave and hurried out. He walked quickly all of that night, glad to be away from the strange place.

Throughout the next day, he slept peacefully on a moss-covered ledge above the sea. Before he fell asleep, he watched a rough-legged hawk circling high above him and heard brown female eider ducks cooing below as they plucked the soft down from their breasts to line the warm nests they were building for their young.

That evening as Tiktaliktak strode along the coast in the soft twilight of the Arctic summer, he saw the rugged coastal mountains sloping gently into the great inland plain. Crossing the foothills, he finally reached the immense plain that stood before his homeland. Now his feet welcomed every step forward in the soft tundra.

The warm sun the next morning followed its course through the eastern sky, and small bright flowers burst into bloom everywhere. The edge of each pond was made beautiful by patches of white Arctic cotton that swayed in the light breeze. Best of all, his namesake, the butterfly, traveled in a straight line before him and seemed to guide him on the long journey homeward.

Now he saw many caribou lying on the hillside with their brown backs blending into the land itself, their antlers covered in thick summer velvet. Tiktaliktak ran for joy to think that he was once again in a place of plenty.

He waded straight across wide shallow lakes, whose water came no higher than his knees, and through streams where every step sent fat sea trout darting away like silver arrows. As he traveled, he crossed high sandy beaches covered with shells, where the sea had washed in ancient times.

At last, he looked across the valley and recognized the three familiar hills that stood before his home—Talliq, Igalaalik, and Aasivak. Soon he would be among his own people. Were they alive? He was almost afraid to know.

He hurried down the gravel slope, across the boulder-strewn floor of the valley that had once been the bed of an immense river, up through the mossy pass between Igalaalik and Aasivak, and up the rise past the small lake where his family took their water for drinking. There lay his sister's sealskin water bucket beside a freshly worn path. They must be living still.

Tiktaliktak sat down beside the path and thought. *If I appear before them quickly, they will think I am a ghost or spirit, for they must surely believe I am dead.*

Getting up, he peered around a large rock down into that beloved valley. There was the big sealskin tent of his family, and beyond it the tent of his uncle, and a little farther up the valley, the family tents of Tauki and Kanguq. Tiktaliktak saw his mother bending over at the entrance to their tent with her head deep in her hood, as was the custom of his people when sad. He saw his sister Saani carrying something that looked like clothing. She took this to her mother, who placed it on a small pile before her. A moment later, Tiktaliktak saw his father step out of their tent and gaze toward the sea.

In the long shadows of early morning, he saw Kanguq and his family, soon followed by the others, walk down toward his father's tent. Although it was not cold, they all had their hoods drawn over their heads in sadness and wore their oldest clothes. Tiktaliktak wondered how he could let them know he had returned without frightening them.

He walked back until he reached the edge of the hill behind the camp, where he knew his figure would be seen easily against the morning sky. Now he moved slowly. Kanguq's sharp eyes saw him first. Tiktaliktak watched him point and call to the others in a low hunter's voice. In a moment, they were all looking at him on the skyline.

"Who is that?" said Kanguq's daughter.

"Can it be?" asked his sister.

"That person has the shape of Tiktaliktak and his way of walking," said Tauki.

Tiktaliktak coughed twice, and they all said, "That is his cough. He coughs in that way."

Then someone said, "Ghost," and another said, "Spirit," and he could see they were all about to run away.

"Relatives," he called in a soft, ordinary voice. "I have returned. I am glad to see you all again." And he sat down on a rock and started to chant and sing a funny little song his mother had taught them as children.

Saani, his sister, called, "Brother of mine, that must be the real you singing that song and no ghost!"

Tiktaliktak answered, "Sister of mine, it is really me. May I come down to you and visit?"

They all began to talk at once. Then Tiktaliktak's father called to him, "Come forward," and he walked out bravely, alone, to meet this ghost, or perhaps his returning son, halfway between the hill and camp.

Tiktaliktak's father looked frightened and suspicious. But coming up to his son, he reached out timidly, touched his arm, and tenderly ran his hand over the great new scars on his son's face. He then passed his hand across his eyes, and feeling tears in them, he leaned forward and gave Tiktaliktak a hug that nearly broke his bones.

In a voice ringing with joy, his father called to his wife and daughters and all the others, saying that this was no ghost but a real person and that, on the very day that they were to give his clothes away, their son at long last had returned home to them.

Tiktaliktak's mother and sisters led him gently into the dark skin tent and seated him on their wide bed made of sweet-smelling summer heather covered with soft, thick winter caribou skins.

They drew off the long, worn-out sealskin boots that he had made and replaced them with warm fur slippers. Slowly, they fed him many of the good things he had dreamed of during his long adventure.

When Tiktaliktak could eat no more, he lay back on the rich warm skins, feeling full of food and contentment. His family was well, and he was overjoyed to be alive and once again in the tent of his father. He closed his eyes and drifted peacefully toward sleep.

In his mind's eye, there arose a shining vision of his island home. Sakkiak now seemed to him a warm and friendly place, for it had become a part of his life, a part of himself.

Tiktaliktak's song floated down to him from the sky. Each word had found its proper place. He could feel himself swaying to the

rhythm of the big drum that beat inside him, and he heard the long answering chorus of women's voices in some distant dance house. His mind, knowing the words, started singing softly:

> Ayii, yaii,
> Ayii, yaii,
> The great sea
> Has set me in motion,
> Set me adrift,
> And I moved
> As a weed moves
> In the river.
>
> The arch of sky
> And mightiness of storms
> Encompassed me,
> And I am left
> Trembling with joy,
> Ayii, yaii,
> Ayii, yaii.

THE WHITE
ARCHER

Kanguq raised his head and listened carefully. Somewhere out in the vast Arctic silence of the Ungava, he had heard a strange sound. He remained kneeling on the scrap of white bearskin, listening, but the sound did not come to him again.

He bent down so that his face was level with the man-sized hole in the ice. Motionless, he watched and waited, peering into the shadowy blue depths of the frozen lake. A short time passed, and then a big trout drifted silently beneath him. Its tail waved gently in the current as it moved its fins like small wings to steady itself. Then another trout glided under him, and behind it three more big ones floated like green ghosts in the icy water.

Tightening his grip on a double-pronged fish spear, Kanguq took careful aim and drove the shaft downward with a lightning thrust. The bone prongs of the spear slipped over the back of the largest fish, and its curved teeth caught and held. Kanguq heaved the struggling fish out of the hole, forced open the prongs of the spear, and released it. The big trout flipped twice on the ice and then lay glazed and still, instantly frozen to death in the intense cold.

Kanguq's sister, Suluk, who had been silently fishing with a short hand line at another hole, came quickly across the snow-covered ice. Kanguq smiled at her as she picked up the huge fish to feel its weight, for it was half as long as she was.

Kanguq's short, strong body was clad in the handsome sealskin parka and pants his mother had made for him. His feet were covered with dark close-fitting sealskin boots that reached his knees. Kanguq's hair was very black, his eyes were dark and lively, and when he smiled, his strong teeth flashed brightly against his dark brown skin.

The evening air around them was still and sharp like thinnest crystal that might break at any moment in the bitter cold. The low white hills beside the frozen lake cast long shadows across the snow, and the winter sky blazed like frozen fire as the sun cast its rays at the first pale shadow of the moon.

Using a bone ladle, Suluk filled a sealskin bucket with water from the hole in the ice and followed her brother across the snow-covered surface of the small lake to the hill that lay above their camp. There, Kanguq put down the heavy trout, and Suluk rested the bucket on the snow. They looked down at the four snowhouses that were the only dwellings in their tiny village. Around the houses many paths curved through the snow. Two long heavy sleds lay upturned, ready for icing, and three delicate skin-covered kayaks rested high on stone racks away from the sharp teeth of the dogs. The igloos seemed deserted except for the dogs scattered around them, and even they lay quietly as though they were carved in stone. Nothing moved. Everything was silent.

"Our family will be glad to taste that fish," said Suluk. "It's the first to be caught during this moon."

Her tawny brown cheeks glowed like the red throat of an Arctic loon, and her long black hair had a blue sheen like the wings of a raven. She was strong and quick, with endless good humor. Her legs were short, but Kanguq knew that she could run like the wind.

As they started down the hill, Kanguq stopped suddenly and stared into the cold blue distance. He pointed up the wide river that curved in a long frozen path from the inland plain through the low hills until it reached their camp by the sea.

"Do you see it?" he asked.

She did not answer. Her eyes searched the vast expanse.

"There it is. Moving. Far up the river. It must be a dog team, but who would be coming from the inland to visit us?" Knowing that their own dogs and sleds were in camp, he said, "They must be strangers from far away. Listen. Listen," he repeated, and faintly, like the measured sound of dripping water somewhere out in the vast silence, they heard the "harr, harr, harr . . ." of a driver urging his dogs forward.

Eager to be the first with news that visitors were coming to their lonely camp, Kanguq and Suluk hurried down the slope to their father's snowhouse.

When it was almost dark, all the men, women, and children of their small village gathered together before the snowhouses in a silent group, ready to meet the strangers. In the half-light they saw a long heavy sled with three men on it swing into view around the river bend. They watched the strange men cross the wind-swept ice and drive their dogs up the steep bank. Two of the men ran beside the sled, working hard to guide it between the boulders that lay exposed on the icy shore. A third man, bigger than the others, remained half sitting, half lying on the sled.

As the strange team rushed into the camp, wild excitement broke loose, and a dog fight started. Everyone helped to kick and pull apart the two powerful teams until finally the dogs settled down, content for the moment to snarl and stiffly circle each other.

Two of the strangers came forward to greet everyone. Rough men they were, with faces burned dark by the wind and cold, eyebrows white with frost. Their fur clothing was worn and torn, which showed they had not had any women's care or mending for a very long time. Their hair was long and black and wildly tangled. With their hoods pushed back and their mitts left carelessly on the sled, they seemed not to notice the cold. One of the men who had run with the sled, a short, strong man, limped a little as though he had lost some toes long ago from freezing.

Kanguq heard his father say to the other driver, a lean man, "I knew you when we were young at the River of Two Tongues. Your father's name was Tunu."

The stranger nodded.

The big man who had remained on the sled raised his left hand in greeting. Kanguq looked at his right arm. It hung limp by his side. Kanguq could see in the fading light that the sleeve of his tattered parka had a long knife slit in it and that his hand was wet with blood.

Because Kanguq's father had known the lean man from the River of Two Tongues, he was bound by politeness to invite the

travelers to sleep in his snowhouse. This he did, and the three men gladly accepted. Kanguq's mother hurried into the igloo and took her proper place near the edge of the sleeping platform beside the lamp, ready to welcome the strangers to their house. Others in the camp unharnessed and fed the visitors' dogs.

The three men tugged off their worn parkas and lay back on the wide sleeping platform, while the women pulled off their seal-skin boots and placed them on the drying rack above the stone lamp filled with seal oil. The big man plucked some soft down from a white bird skin that lay near the lamp and carefully placed it against the long knife wound to stop the bleeding. A seal was cut open for them and prepared for feasting. They greedily drank quantities of fresh cold water and some hot blood soup. After the feast of delicious seal meat, which they had eaten raw, sliced thin, half thawed and half frozen, they lay back in the welcome warmth of

the igloo and talked to Kanguq's father. The people from the other igloos gathered to hear the news. Everyone listened.

The lean man from the River of Two Tongues recounted their long sled journey. He told of their travels through the range of coastal hills onto the great wind-swept plain in search of caribou. For weeks they had seen nothing but one half-starved wolf. Fierce blizzards had raged inland, and they had gone hungry. Their only food had come from the few ptarmigan they managed to catch. When this news was told, the listeners nodded, for they also knew those small white furry-footed birds inhabiting the inland plain. Their flesh had saved the lives of many travelers. Finally the three men had been forced to eat one of their own dogs, but some time after that they saw a few caribou tracks on the very edge of the Land of Little Sticks.

There they stopped, for it was tree country, dreaded territory belonging to the First Nations. The dwarfed trees that grew there were permanently bent by the icy blasts of the north wind. They were few and scattered, and scarcely any of them was taller than a man. There was little soil, and only tundra moss grew there, clinging tightly to the rocks. The Land of Little Sticks was a terrible land, feared by the birds and beasts of the true forest and shunned by the animals that roved the open plain. It was a starving land. Three stone images built to stand like men marked this place. To the south, on the distant horizon, lay vast forest and lake country, a land that suffered a short hot summer alive with black flies and mosquitoes that could drive a man mad.

Inuit feared the people of the First Nations. The harnesses of their dog teams became entangled in these little stick trees. Ancient

Inuit stories told of terrifying nights spent there, for the wind made the trees moan and whisper like lost souls. Cruel warriors were said to live and hide in this tree country, and no Inuk considered himself safe there.

Yet the hunger pangs of these three men were so terrible that they overcame all their fear and traveled on and on up the narrow frozen river between the sharp-pointed shadows of the little stick trees. When they climbed a hill to look out over the country for signs of caribou, the big man pointed to a thin wisp of smoke rising in the cold, still air. Frightened they were, but starving as well, and they drew closer until they smelled boiling meat.

The big man, made bold with hunger, left his two hunting companions and the dogs behind and stalked alone through the dreaded trees until he reached a rise in the ground where he could watch the camp. He was careful to stay downwind so that the dogs could not smell him and warn their First Nations masters of his presence. He remained there, hiding and watching, from noon until the evening sky turned red. Then he retraced his steps to tell the other two men that the camp was small, having only one tall man, one very old man, a woman, a girl, and two young children. The camp, he said, had only four dogs, which were so small that they looked like starved black foxes. Besides the dogs, they had only one toboggan and a small skin tent hung on poles. But they also had some frozen caribou meat tied up in the trees, safe from their hungry dogs, and rich otter skins stretched on wooden frames for drying.

"I am going to take some of that meat tonight," he said to his companions, "for I am starving."

Pointing to the southeast, his companions replied, "We saw the smoke of ten fires rising beyond those hills, and we heard the sounds of countless dogs fighting. We warn you, there lies a large camp."

"I care nothing about them," said the big man. "I must have food or else I will die. Will you come with me tonight?"

The two hunters were frightened, but because there was only one sled, there was no way for them to part, and so they finally agreed to go with him. That night when they had carefully anchored the dogs by turning the heavy sled over, they set out for the small camp. In single file they moved cautiously through the dreaded, unfamiliar country. It was deathly cold, and the stars seemed to wheel and dance overhead. The night sky glowed with eerie green northern lights that magically shifted and faded like underwater weeds waving in a river. The trees in the forest cracked loudly with the frost, and dry powder snow, lying on the branches, showered down on the men without warning. All of these things made them nervous, angry, and afraid.

At last they saw the yellow glow of firelight from within a strange tent, and the big man, again smelling the rich odor of cooking meat, went forward at once. The other two remained at the edge of the clearing. For some time there was silence. Then a dog barked, and then another, and they could hear a man's voice shouting excitedly in a strange language. There was a woman's high-pitched scream and the sound of fighting and more dogs barking. The big man's voice then called to them, shouting their names again and again, and they both ran forward. Their coming must have frightened the camp, for they saw no one except the big man,

who came stumbling through the soft snow carrying the double haunches of a caribou. They saw his knife glistening in the starlight, and there was blood spattered on his clothing.

They turned and ran hard until they reached their sled, and all that night they drove the dogs along the frozen river until they were safely out of the Land of Little Sticks. In the morning they rested briefly and ate their fill of the stolen caribou meat, giving most of the remainder to their starving dogs. Then they hurried on. They followed the wide flat river course toward the coast and the safety of other Inuit camps, but they did not return to their own camp at the River of Two Tongues. They knew that the First Nations would not venture far from the Land of Little Sticks, for they hated and feared the great treeless, barren land where they could find no wood for their fires nor lodge poles for their tents and became lost traveling in endless circles out on the terrible wind-swept plain.

Kanguq's father looked at the three men after he had heard their story and said nothing. In his view they had acted foolishly to be caught starving in the Land of Little Sticks, and certainly they should not have stolen or acted violently. They had broken the laws of the Inuit.

The family and the three unwanted guests drifted off into an uneasy sleep only to be awakened twice by the big man who cried out in pain, perhaps because of the knife wound in his arm or because of some terrible dream that had come to haunt him from the First Nations camp.

The next day the three men stayed on the sleeping platform until noon, and although they were not offered food, they made no plans to leave. The big man sat sullen and silent, holding his right arm as he rocked back and forth to ease the pain. His arm and hand had swollen in the night.

The three visitors prepared to spend the second night, and Kanguq's father again gave them food. But this time they all ate in silence.

When his father went out of the snowhouse after eating, Kanguq followed him, and they stood together in the cold star-filled night. They listened carefully. The father looked up the river from whence the three men had come. He thought of their sled tracks, of their footprints, and even of the drops of blood from the big man's arm that all led straight to the camp. They had left a trail in the snow that even a child could follow. Kanguq's father looked at him in a worried way, and Kanguq felt the hair stir on the back of his neck, for he knew that the people from the Land of Little Sticks would have good reason to be angry.

Neither Kanguq nor his father had ever seen these strangers, although his father had once passed one of their campsites on the edge of the barrens. There he had seen a dead fire and the cleared place where they had pitched their strange tents. Bones and feathers were scattered everywhere, and the smell of smoked skins still lingered in the damp tundra moss.

Kanguq followed his father back inside the snowhouse, where the three men were already asleep. Kanguq's mother smiled at her husband and son as she trimmed the wick in her seal-oil lamp until it caused a gentle glow to reflect from the glistening snow walls. She then arranged the boots on the rack over the lamp so they would be dry in the morning.

On this night Kanguq slept in his clothes with his head toward the foot of the sleeping platform, which is sometimes the custom of young boys when the only bed of the house is crowded with guests. He slowly drifted off to sleep and dreamed of peering through the hole in the lake ice, where he saw a hidden world wrapped in green shadows with fishlike people swimming among strange houses that looked like igloos piled one upon the other.

Suddenly he awoke. What he saw was not a dream. Strange men with dark hats were crowding into the low entrance of the snowhouse, filling the room with their harsh words and violent movements. He saw a knife flash. Then someone kicked over the lamp. In the dark there was angry shouting, screaming, and the sound of stabbing. Kanguq jumped up as he felt a sharp cut on his ankle. Clinging to the wall, he crouched down and felt his way around the edge of the house until he came to the entrance. Bending low, he rushed past a tall, gaunt man who smelled of smoke. The man tried to grab him as he ran out into the night, but he was able to break away. Where could he go? The house was full of fear, of shouting, of words and sounds he had never heard before.

Kanguq ran past the neighboring igloo and beyond the rack of kayaks until he reached the snowhouse of his uncle and aunt. They were both sitting up in bed, terrified by the sounds they heard. They quickly grabbed him and hid him under the thick pile of caribou skins on the bed, and then they lay on top of him. He heard running footsteps and more strange voices. A man rushed in looking for him, but seeing only two old people in bed, the stranger grunted with disgust and hurried out again.

When the first light of day allowed them to see, Kanguq poked a small hole in the wall of his uncle's snowhouse and looked toward his father's igloo. One wall had been broken in, and their household things were scattered everywhere. He saw no movement.

In front of the house he counted eleven raiders. Tall, thin men they were, with faces made terrible by painted black streaks. They were wearing strange pointed hats and long coats with weird markings. Each man carried a bow or club or knife in his hand. They were calling to each other in excited voices. Several of them were shooting arrows into the igloo and into the bearskin and two sealskins that were stretched out to dry. With their knives they had slashed the pelts and cut the sealskin dog lines into pieces. They had pulled the kayaks from their racks, had ripped them open, and had smashed their long, delicate frames. They were gathering all the food they could find, and they were preparing to go.

Suddenly Kanguq caught a glimpse of his sister, Suluk. He watched with terror as the men led her down toward one of their toboggans on the river.

Then as dawn turned the village gray, they started to search the other igloos again. Kanguq's aunt quickly made him put on her long-tailed woman's parka and handed him a skin bucket. Disguised as an old woman, he bent over, his head hidden deep in the hood, and hobbled away from the igloo. He went off toward the side of the village as though he were going to the lake to get water. Halfway through the camp he saw one of the visitors, the big man, lying face down on the snow with two arrows in his back, his bloody arm flung out stiffly before him.

Out of the corner of his eye, Kanguq saw one of the raiders point at him and another place an arrow in his bow and take aim. The arrow whistled past his face and buried itself in the snow. Fortunately he did not aim again. Kanguq hobbled over the hill beyond their sight. Once at the lake, he threw off his aunt's parka and snatched up a broken ivory-bladed snow knife that lay by a hole in the ice. Then he ran.

He ran as far and as fast as he could. He headed northward, following the coastline so he would not lose his way. Far up beyond the River of Giant Men, he knew there were Inuit who would help him.

When night came, he struggled to find strength to go on. He lay in the snow, exhausted, and his eyes filled with tears as he thought of the fate of his mother and father, his relatives, and his sister, Suluk. Then slowly a terrible anger started to grow within him. Dark thoughts rushed through his mind. He had only twelve winters of life upon him, but if he could live to reach the next Inuit camp, he swore inside himself that he would avenge the terrible wrong done his family by the people from the Land of Little Sticks. He pounded the hard snow with his fists and swore this to himself, again and again.

He was afraid to build a snowhouse for fear he might be followed, and when he had rested a little, he went on despite the darkness, because he knew that if he slept without shelter, he would freeze to death. To avoid leaving a trail, he traveled along wind-packed drifts that were so hard his footsteps left no mark.

Worn out and starving and driven by fear, he slowly made his way north. After the first night he cut blocks out of the frozen snow and piled them in a circle to form a house scarcely big enough for a dog. Some nights it was so cold that he could not sleep, but the little houses protected him against the biting wind that swept in from the frozen sea, and he was able to stay alive. He lost count of the number of snowhouses he built and the days he limped through the killing cold. The knife slash in his ankle pained him.

One evening, a seal hunter called Inukpak, returning to his camp after hunting out on the sea ice, saw the boy staggering half frozen among the ice hummocks near the shore. He carried Kanguq to his sled, wrapped him in a caribou skin, and put his arm around his shoulders to steady him. Inukpak got the boy safely back to camp, where his wife put him into the center of their warm bed and fed him hot blood soup and little pieces of rich seal meat. She cared for him like a mother until he was well and strong again.

For two long years he stayed with Inukpak and his wife, watching and waiting as each season advanced across the land. He searched for eggs and fished with the other young people of the camp, but there was a dark and fearful quietness that seemed to brood inside him. He never spoke of the fate of his parents, or of his sister, or of the people of the Little Sticks, but they were always in his mind.

In the late autumn of the second year, after the first big snow had turned everything white so that the dog teams could travel again, a hunter came with his son from a camp farther to the north. One evening he told a long story of a visit he had made to a distant island that could only be reached by sled during the two moons of midwinter. There he had met a strange old man full of mystery, with a knowledge of the ways of men and animals. His eyes and body seemed weak, but he could draw a huge horn bow that the strongest man among them could not even bend, and his old eyes could still see well enough to drive an arrow straight to its mark no matter how far or how small. His wife, it was said, could hand-stitch the seams of a kayak with sinew so that no water could ever enter, and she could so tightly sew a cut in a man's skin that one could never see the stitches. Their only sadness, said the hunter, was that they had no children. The old man had said that he would soon go blind.

During the night, Kanguq thought about all that he had heard, and in the morning he said to Inukpak and his wife, "I give thanks to you for your kindness, for you have saved my life and been a family to me. But now I wish to travel north with that man who visits and his son, if they will take me, for I long to see that old man on the island and talk with him."

Inukpak said that he would be glad if Kanguq would stay in their camp and be a son to them. But Kanguq only thanked them again and said once more that he wished to go north.

The visiting seal hunter agreed to take Kanguq to his camp, and so they set out one dark and windy morning in early winter when the snow was hard and the sled could move fast. Inukpak's wife had made Kanguq new sealskin boots and mitts. She gave them to him for the journey, and Inukpak gave him two seals, one to help feed the dogs on the trip north and one as a gift for the people in the new camp.

After saying farewell, they traveled north for five days, following the coast through a frozen empty land. During their journey they crossed only one fox track and saw no other sign of life save two thin ravens that croaked loudly as they chased and tumbled with each other across the evening sky.

On the fifth night Kanguq saw the glow of lights from the ice windows of the three snowhouses in the seal hunter's camp, and the dogs raced forward, delighted to be home at last. Everyone came out to welcome the returning travelers, and they showed Kanguq every sign of friendship.

The long, hard snowdrifts were driven high against the hills, and Kanguq waited patiently for the midwinter moons when the weather would be even colder and the sea frozen hard, and when the sun would not light the river valleys.

The seal hunter knew that to go to the island was very important to Kanguq, and for this reason he planned to make the trip. His wife was worried, for she knew the danger of crossing by sled from the mainland to the island because the great tides could at any moment tear out the ice bridge between the two. When they were preparing to make the perilous journey, she begged her husband not to take their son, for she feared that they might both be lost to her, and to this he agreed.

Kanguq helped the hunter ice the lightest and fastest sled in the camp, spitting a mouthful of water along the upturned runners and polishing it into icy smoothness with a scrap of bearskin. The other hunters lent the seal hunter their strongest dogs so that the sled would go swiftly, and they loaded it with nothing save two thick fur sleeping skins, a harpoon, a snow knife, and a seal for food.

They traveled north along the coast and slept three nights on the way. Then they turned outward on the frozen sea, and Kanguq realized the terrible hazards that lay before them. The barren rock island was hidden from view, wrapped in whirling drifts of snow. Dark patches of open water and frightening black holes showed dangerously against the whiteness of the snow-covered ice. In the bitter cold these open holes threw up gray fog against the darkened sky, and mists froze and fell back like snow into the black water. Many times the hunter had to walk before the dogs, feeling with his harpoon for a safe passage across the treacherous sea ice that was broken by the rising and falling tides.

At last Kanguq saw stretching out toward the island a great ice bridge, and they started along this narrow strip. But soon it grew dark and the wind rose, and they were forced to stop for the night. There was no snow there to build an igloo, just naked ice, and the howling wind swept down from the north with increasing fury. The hunter and Kanguq turned their sled on its side to give them protection against the wind and rolled themselves up in the sleeping skins. With the dogs huddled around them, they managed to stay alive. Kanguq lay shivering, listening in fear and wonder to the great sighing of the new-formed ice. If the ice bridge broke, they would drown in the freezing waters.

As if by magic, in the early morning the wind died, and the hunter sat up and looked around him. The air was still now, and the whirling snow had faded away.

There, plainly visible, lay the island, known as Tujjaq. It was high and rocky, the point of a hidden mountain thrusting its stone head out of the frozen sea. Only in one place were the sheer rock walls broken by a narrow cleft. Around the island was a huge ice

ledge, and beyond this was a rough broken collar of ice chunks that rose and fell with the moving tides. Snow filled every crack in the dark rocks, but the hard, smooth places were all blown clear by the savage winds that roared over the island.

The hunter drove his team along the ice ledge on the south face of the island cliffs toward the narrow opening in the rock wall. The entrance to the steep passage stood before them like a needle's eye. They began the climb, and so hard was the ascent that they often had to help the dogs to find footing. At length they reached a narrow slit in the top of the cliff. It led into a huge round place surrounded by rust-colored granite walls rising higher than a man could throw a stone. It was roofless—and so wide that Kanguq thought he could not cross it in a hundred leaps. At the base of this

stone room, there were many entrances into dark caves and passages, and higher up among the steep, smooth rocks, there were narrow walks and holes in the stone wall that looked like windows.

Kanguq followed the hunter forward across the open, snow-carpeted area until they came to a small house half buried in the ground, with walls that were shoulder high and made of stone. The roof beams of the house were the ribs of whales, covered with large sealskins weighted in place with a thick layer of sod. On either side of the entrance stood the great jawbones of a whale.

As they peered at this strange entrance, wondering what to do, a dwarf man pushed aside the sealskin curtain that served as a door for the house and waved them inside. He had powerful arms and shoulders and a twisted back, and his hair was long and knotted in the ancient style. He smiled at them in a shy and kindly way when they entered.

It was dark inside the little stone house, and Kanguq crouched in the entrance passage, waiting for his eyes to become accustomed to the light. He saw the old woman first as she sat tending her stone lamp that was shaped like a half-moon. It burned with an even white flame, reflecting across the pool of rich seal fat that was its fuel. The old woman nodded and smiled and beckoned at them to come and sit beside her on the sleeping platform.

Kanguq observed her carefully. Her warm brown face was flat and wide, with powerful jaw muscles that drew the flesh tight over her high cheekbones. Her eyes were jet black, and as she looked at Kanguq again, they shone warmly, revealing all the hidden power of life within her. Her eyelids had been drawn narrow by a whole lifetime in the wind and snow and sun. Around her eyes and mouth and spreading up across her forehead, there appeared countless tiny wrinkles like the fine grain in an ancient piece of driftwood. When she smiled, her strong white teeth clamped together, worn evenly from chewing and softening numberless sealskins. Her hair, black and much thinner now than when she had been a girl, was caught in two tight braids that coiled neatly around her ears. Not one gray hair showed.

Bending forward, the old woman made a seat for Kanguq, and he noticed that her short body, like her eyes, gave him the feeling of someone with quickness and hidden strength. Her round brown wrists had delicate blue tattooing on them, which had been done for her when she was a child. Her hands were strong and square. The right thumb and forefinger were bent and powerful from forcing bone needles through thick animal skins.

Kanguq was startled when he sat down. He had not noticed beside her the old man kneeling on the sleeping platform. This ancient Inuk was as motionless as though he were carved of stone. The light from the lamp did not seem to touch him, and he remained wrapped in shadows.

"My husband has been away in the storm," said the old woman. "Now he is back and resting. He will wake soon. You two have had a long trip and must be hungry."

She waved to the dwarf, who placed horn bowls of melted ice water, a dark red saddle of young walrus meat, and sun-dried strips of trout before them, and the hunter and Kanguq ate quickly. Then the old woman cleverly drew the flame along the lamp's wick until it made the whole house glow with a soft, even light.

When Kanguq was filled, he wiped his hands and mouth with a soft bird skin. He stole another glance at the old man, who remained motionless in the same position. But now the ancient wrinkled face and hands seemed to glow like ivory, and there was light around the old man's long white hair and the thin traces of his beard. His eyelids fluttered and opened, he slowly turned his head, and he looked at Kanguq with eyes that were dark green and shadowy like pools of water on the sea ice.

"You have arrived," he said in a deep voice that made Kanguq know he must be a great singer.

"Yes, we have arrived," answered Kanguq in the most formal manner, for he felt both fear and respect for this old man.

"You have had a long journey, and now it is time for you both to sleep," said the old man. "I shall think a while on what will be best for you now that you are here. Sleep," he said again, "sleep."

The seal hunter and Kanguq lay back on the soft caribou furs, glad to be safe in the warmth of this old stone house. Kanguq looked up and wondered at the mighty ribs that curved across the low ceiling, and as he drifted off to sleep, he imagined himself inside the living body of a whale as it plunged into the depths of the sea.

When he awoke the next morning, light streamed down through the thin, transparent window above the door. The window was made of stretched seal intestine carefully sewn together by the old woman and was the only source of daylight in the house. Kanguq sat up quickly when he realized that the seal hunter had already gone.

"He left very early," said the old woman, nodding above her

lamp. "He wished to cross the ice bridge while the weather remained fair and the wind gentle. He asked me to say farewell to you. My husband, Ittuq, has gone out, too, for he has always loved to watch the dawning of each new day."

Kanguq bent low at the small entrance, and once outside, he breathed deeply in the clear, sharp air. No one was in sight. He looked up at the pale light of day brightening the eastern sky, and then he noticed a movement in one of the entrances in the rock wall. The old man walked slowly out into the daylight. He leaned heavily on the powerful dwarf, one arm draped across the little man's hunched shoulders. As they made their way toward him, Kanguq noticed in the old man's free hand a great thick bow.

"You have come to learn, and I am here to teach," said the old man, in his deep rich voice. "This," he added, holding up the bow, "this is Kiggavik, the dark falcon, swiftest hunter of them all."

He placed one end of the bow against the frozen ground, and with a swift, powerful downward motion, he bent it and slipped the bowstring over the end notch. This bow was of a size and strength that Kanguq had never known. It was made of musk-ox horn from the Inuit place they call the Land Behind the Sun. It was polished smooth and bound in many places with the finest braided caribou sinew. Best of all, it was beautifully shaped, swept back like the outstretched wings of a plunging falcon. Never had there been such a bow.

Ittuq offered it to Kanguq, who held it in his hands like a precious treasure. He placed his hand on the string, and the touch made it sing like the east wind.

"Now, draw the bow," said the old man.

Kanguq drew back hard, but the braided sinew did not move.

"Draw the bow," said Ittuq once again.

It would not move.

"Draw the bow," Ittuq commanded.

Taking a deep breath and using all his strength, Kanguq managed to draw it back until it reached its full curve.

"Look! See that! See!" the old man called out in excitement to the dwarf. "You who can crack stones with your teeth and break the back of a white bear with your strong arms cannot draw that bow. But this boy, he can draw the bow. He can make the falcon sing. Look. He will be an archer. Perhaps he will be a great archer. Tomorrow our long task will begin."

Together, Kanguq and the dwarf helped Ittuq back into the house, where they carefully unstrung Kiggavik and wrapped it safely in soft skins. Kanguq's hands trembled as he looked at the great bow and thought of the fate of his family. *Revenge! Revenge! With a bow such as this I could have revenge!* The thought cut through him like a cruel wind.

That evening they picked rich marrow from the soft centers of caribou bones and ate the sweet flesh of young sea birds that had been preserved in seal oil. When the feast was over, the old man lay back among the thick caribou skins and went to sleep, and the dwarf left the small house for the freezing caves where he slept.

Kanguq watched the old woman sew a new pair of sealskin boots. Her stitches were so small that he could not see them. She asked him about his mother, and slowly he told her the story of his life, which until now he had told no one. He spoke of his love for his parents and his sister, Suluk, and of that terrible night when the invaders had come, the night when his whole life had changed. Though he had never before revealed his innermost feelings, he told the old woman every hidden thought within him, every hate and joy, fear and longing. To Kanguq she did not seem like other people. She was somehow like the earth itself. Speaking with her, he had the same feeling he had when he lay on soft tundra, warmed by the summer sun, and looked up at the wide blue sky. Then he felt he could understand every word of the wind's song. She was that kind of person.

When he had told her everything, he felt a great relief and went to sleep immediately. The old woman rose stiffly from her place on the sleeping platform and gently spread a warm caribou skin over her old husband and the young sleeping boy. Then she returned to her sewing.

During the late winter moon, the dwarf, whose name Taliqjuaq means "big arms," told Kanguq many things about their island home. He showed him the way through the numerous passages inside the granite cliffs that surrounded the little house, and the place where he, Taliqjuaq, slept. It was a small stone room, icy cold, with nothing in it save the skin of a huge white bear that lay neatly folded on a rock ledge that served as his bed. He showed Kanguq the two rear entrances to the caves. One led to the small deep lake where they got fresh water; the other opened at the place where the dogs were kept. Beyond the high rock, the island of Tujjaq stretched north, and there they often walked along the cliffs, scanning the frozen sea, looking for walrus or whales in the big open pools of water.

From the time of his arrival, Kanguq helped Taliqjuaq to feed and care for the ten strong sled dogs. The dwarf taught him how to rule the big dogs without fear and to respect the white female lead dog named Lau. It was she who led the strong team and responded quickly to the driver's orders. She was not the strongest fighter, but she was always protected by the biggest male dog in the team. Lau soon began to rub her thick white coat against Kanguq's leg and to lick his hands when he came to feed her.

One winter night when the air was still and cold and the moon rose up bone-white and calm as a sleeper's face, Kanguq heard the long, lonely howl of a white wolf far away on the other end of the island, where rocky crags plunged straight down to the frozen sea. The eerie sound came to him again and again, and he heard Lau answer the white wolf with a high moaning that he had never known before.

Kanguq hurried to the sheltered place where the dog team slept, but Lau was already gone. She was running fast across the hard-packed snow toward the far end of the island. When he turned to enter the passage again, he found Taliqjuaq standing beside him.

"That big white wolf will kill your little Lau," said Taliqjuaq. But he was wrong.

The next day Kanguq found Lau back with the team. She seemed tired from her long run but contented. Later, in the spring, Lau grew big, and Kanguq built a small snowhouse for her.

One morning he heard her snarling viciously at the other dogs, and looking into her small house, he found that she had eight new-born pups. All of them were white as snow. She let Kanguq pick one up to examine it. It had a longer muzzle and larger ears than a husky. Its legs were long and thin, and its feet splayed wide, which would be good for running swiftly on the snow. This was no ordinary pup that Kanguq held. It was half wolf and half dog.

Kanguq hurried back to the house to tell the news to Ittuq and the old woman.

Laughing with delight, the old man said, "If you can raise those children of the white wolf, they will be yours. Wolves are not as strong as dogs, but they are fast and tireless and need little food."

Soon after, the dwarf appeared and spread a large scraped seal-skin on the edge of the sleeping platform. On this he placed some long caribou rib bones and a pile of strong sinews that had been drawn from a caribou's back. Beside these he laid several short knives, a sharpening stone, and two special pieces of bone, one for straightening arrows and the other for bending the bow.

Then the old man and the boy began their long task. Slowly they shaped and matched the strong springy rib bones and cut them so they fit together perfectly into one piece to make a delicate curving bow.

While they worked, the old woman sat silently by her lamp, and with skilled hands she spread the sinews apart with a little horn comb. Then she spun and knotted them between her nimble fingers until they became long strands of strong brown thread. These she braided together into thin cords. They were each as fine as a

single blade of grass, and yet they could easily carry the whole weight of a man. She dampened these cords with snow water and handed them to the old man, who slowly bound each piece of bone in place with the sinew cords. He then ran the cords up and down along the whole length of the bow many times until the strands lay evenly together. These strands he bound tightly to the bow. When the cords dried, they gripped the bow like a falcon's claw and gave springing power to it.

Now the old woman handed them the strongest double-braided strand of all, the bowstring itself, made from the center sinew of a bull caribou's back. When the bone bow was flexed and the bowstring gripped the notch, it drew all the long sinews tight and gave added strength. The bow was much smaller than the great Kiggavik and felt lighter in Kanguq's hand. It was white like a young falcon. It was made for him, and he wished more than anything to become skilled with it quickly.

A few days later when the bow was finished, they began to make the arrows. The old man took long pieces of caribou bone, split them, shaped them, and bound them together. At the end of each shaft he made a slit, and into this he forced a slim stone arrowhead made of hardest slate. The old man had shown Kanguq how to shape and sharpen each head. At the other end of each arrow, after it was notched, they bound the dark wing feathers of a raven to the shaft to guide the arrow in its flight.

When their work was finished, the old woman handed Kanguq a trim quiver made of sealskin with two compartments, one for the new bow and the other for the arrows.

The long white Arctic spring faded as the sun of summer

wheeled above the island. Everywhere the soft gray tundra moss appeared through the snow, and the tiny Arctic flowers unfolded like colored stars. Small birds returned from warm lands in the south and sang their songs as they hopped about gathering dried moss for their nests. The weather softened, and warm mists rose in the early mornings. It was a joy to hear the faint bird sounds after the long silence of winter, for it was as though the whole world were being born again. The sun never left the sky.

"Set up a target, boy," said the old man early one morning. "It is time you learned to use the new bow."

In great excitement Kanguq ran out and hurriedly built up two targets with the last soft snow that remained against the north wall hidden from the sun. One target was a model of a bear, the other the likeness of a man.

When Kanguq returned to the little house, the old man and the dwarf were waiting for him.

"Are you an enemy of all white bears?" asked the old man.

Kanguq thought about this question for a moment.

"No," he answered, "but I hope that one day a white bear will offer himself to me."

"Then do not drive arrows into his image or all white bears will be offended. And men, Kanguq, would you do harm to all men?"

"No," said Kanguq quickly. "I seek eleven bowmen. Those will I harm. Those I will kill."

"Hear me well, Kanguq," Ittuq said. "Do not give men cause to fear you, for one who does that is no better than a dog gone mad, wishing only to bite and kill."

Ittuq waved his hand, and the dwarf hobbled across and cut out two large square blocks of snow, placed one upon the other, and in the center of the upper block stuck a dark piece of tundra moss about the size of a man's hand.

The old man stepped forward. He took Kanguq's new bow and stood for a moment as though he were in deep thought. Then scarcely looking at the target, he aimed, drew back the bowstring, and released it. Although he had not placed an arrow in the bow, he said to Taliqjuaq that he was out of practice and had missed the mark.

Again the old man seemed lost in thought, and again he drew the bow without an arrow. He released the bowstring and said that this time he had struck the mark.

"Now, Kanguq, it is your turn."

Kanguq raised the bow, aimed, quickly drew back the empty bowstring, and released it.

The old man stepped forward beside him and said, "You must learn to shoot the bow and guide the arrows with your mind, for it is only with the power of your thoughts that you will become a great archer. Imagine that you have a true arrow. Draw and release it, and guide it quickly with your eye and mind straight to the mark."

Kanguq concentrated, drawing the bow again and again without using an arrow.

"Now practice each day," commanded Ittuq. "Practice until your mind is tired and your fingers bleed on the bowstring, and at the end of summer I shall let you use one of your arrows."

Kanguq's mind flashed backward to the dreaded scene that haunted him, waking or sleeping—the scene of his father's broken snowhouse and his sister being taken away. He gripped his throat to keep from screaming out in anger. He must do as the old one commanded.

During the short summer Kanguq practiced long and hard. Sometimes he saw the old man and the dwarf watching him from the entrance of the dark caves, but they said not a word.

One morning when he awoke there was a light fall of snow on the ground, almost covering the autumn red of the tundra, and the little ponds were covered with a thin sheet of ice.

When he went outside with his bow, the old man and Taliqjuaq were waiting for him. Ittuq handed him a single arrow. Black feathered it was and long, with a sharp tip. Kanguq felt a surge of wild excitement as he placed the arrow in his bow. He aimed at the small target of woven hide and released the arrow. It flew wide of the mark and struck harmlessly in the tundra.

"Bring it back quickly," cried the old man, and Kanguq ran across the wide space and returned with the arrow.

"Now, think," said Ittuq. "Think what you are trying to do. Guide the arrow with your eye. Force it with your mind to go straight to the mark."

Kanguq drew the bow again and held it until it seemed to him that the feathered shaft reached in and touched the very center of his being. Then he released the arrow, and it flew straight down the course, following his line of vision until it struck the center of the target.

"Good!" shouted the old man, and Taliqjuaq smiled and nodded his head at Kanguq. "You have it now. Practice with that black

arrow until the midwinter moon and I, an old man, shall take you hunting."

After they had gone, Kanguq stood alone surrounded by the great stone walls and thought again, fiercely, of why he wanted to be a great bowman. Only he could avenge the wrong done to his family. Concentrating once more, he raised the bow and with an easy rhythm drove the arrow straight through the heavy target.

Slowly winter came to them, and it was dark until noon each day. Savage winds blew in from the frozen sea and seemed to hold the land in an icy grasp. A new bridge of ice formed solidly between the mainland and their island home. The old woman had completed her work on their winter clothes, and Taliqjuaq had prepared the long sled and harnesses for the big dogs. They were ready for the journey.

They planned to leave Lau on the island to fend for her growing family of young white wolf dogs, knowing she would teach them to dig beneath the snow for lemming and to catch hare and ptarmigan to feed themselves.

On a clear day Taliqjuaq loaded the sled down on the sea ice. Kanguq and the old woman helped Ittuq down the high snowy passage from their home. Once they were on the sled, Kanguq was surprised at Ittuq's agility. He sat beside his wife, and although his eyes and legs were weak, his arms were strong, and he rode the sled cleverly, balancing and shifting his weight as they crossed the rough ice. Ittuq called commands to the new lead dog in his deep songlike voice, and the dog obeyed instantly. Kanguq and the powerful dwarf sat on the long sled or ran beside it, guiding it across the snow.

That night they slept near the end of the ice bridge, close to the land, where snow had drifted. The dwarf and Kanguq built a new igloo, and when it was completed, the old woman hurried inside to spread the sleeping skins neatly over the snow bench. She took a live spark from a small stone tinder box that she carried when traveling, blew it into a flame, and lighted the wick in her little seal-oil lamp.

When the dogs were fed and the men entered the igloo, they placed the thick snow door neatly over the entrance and ate some tasty strips of seal meat. The old woman pulled off their boots and placed them carefully on the drying rack over the lamp. She looked around her new house and saw the white walls glistening like diamonds. She laughed out loud with pleasure, for she loved to travel.

The next day they journeyed beyond the ice of the sea and moved inland, following a flat river course through the coastal hills. The wind blew violently, and that night they built a strong igloo in the protection of the riverbank. Snow whipped into the air until they could not see each other or the dogs, and they were forced to remain in this snowhouse for three days until the storm died.

When they went out once more into the fresh white world, their dogs were buried deeply in the snow, sleeping comfortably in the warmth of their heavy fur coats with their tails curled above their noses so they could breathe.

Now they traveled for five long days across the white flatness of the inland plain, where land and sky were joined together in a long

unbroken line. Sometimes on a wind-swept place the old man told Kanguq to set up one stone upon another to mark the trail so that they could trace their way back out of the flat land in case they ever came this way again. On the fourth day they crossed a few caribou tracks, and on the fifth day there were a great many fresh tracks.

They stopped early in the afternoon and built a snowhouse larger than the others of the trip, and on its front they built a small meat porch. This igloo had a clear ice window over the door and a long tunnel entrance to keep out the wind, as they expected to stay here for some time.

The old woman started fixing the inside of the new house, beating the snow out of the sleeping skins to make them dry and comfortable. Kanguq heard her singing to herself an ancient song as she lighted the flame of her lamp:

"Ayii, Ayii,
Even as a spirit
Joyfully I'll roam
Down every river valley
That leads toward the sea.
Ayii, Ayii."

That night as they lay among the furs on the sleeping bench, they began to talk. This was the time Kanguq liked best, for it was a time to speak, to listen, and to learn. The old man said to Kanguq, "Being a hunter is many things. To be a clever bowman is not enough. First you must know where to find the animals, and then when you have found them, you must know how to stalk them on this flat plain or out on the open ice of the sea. A man does not just kill because he is a clever hunter. He succeeds in the hunt only if he is a good man, a wise man, who obeys the rules of life. If the animals or birds or fish see that a man is cruel and stupid, they will not give themselves to him.

"Tomorrow, if the weather is good," continued Ittuq, "you will hunt with Taliqjuaq. He is slow with his legs, but he has become wise with his mind. Do not take a bow or spear with you. Taliqjuaq does not need such weapons, for he was born among the caribou people and he knows many ways to stalk the animals on the plain."

In the morning, the dwarf and Kanguq dressed in their warmest caribou skin clothing, for a light wind was blowing out of the west and it was bitter cold. Kanguq shyly handed a pair of wooden snow goggles to Taliqjuaq, for he had carved two pairs of narrow-slitted goggles during the long blizzard. Taliqjuaq thanked him and said that now they would not go blind in the glaring whiteness. Taliqjuaq rolled two skins tightly and tied them across his back, and he showed Kanguq how to place a long knife inside his skin boot.

After walking some distance, they came to a slight rise in the ground. The dwarf quickly led Kanguq up it, hobbling very fast with his short broken way of hop-walking. When they were on the highest ground, the dwarf showed Kanguq how to hold his mittened hands together. Taliqjuaq then hopped up lightly into Kanguq's hands and stepped onto his shoulders. From this height he searched the country with his hawklike eyes and then quickly hopped down.

Kanguq looked around carefully and said, "I see nothing."

"Come with me," said Taliqjuaq. "Just beyond the river there are as many caribou as I have fingers and toes. They are difficult to see when they are lying down, for their backs are almost white with frost from their breathing."

The dwarf then led Kanguq on a long walk across the plain.

"Are we near them now?" whispered Kanguq while searching hard with his eyes.

"No. We are farther from them," said Taliqjuaq. "But we are downwind of them, and they will not smell us here. Sit down and rest."

Taliqjuaq quickly spread one caribou skin over his shoulders and sat down on the lowest part. Kanguq did the same with the other skin.

"Look," the dwarf whispered. "They're up and moving, feeding at that place where the wind has blown the tundra clear of snow."

For the first time, Kanguq saw the caribou, twenty of them, pale as silver ghosts, blending with the snow and sky.

Taliqjuaq rose slowly, and bending over, he blew his breath across the dark hairs of the skin so that frost formed and made the skin silvery and difficult to see. It looked exactly like the caribou before them. Then he drew the soft hide around his shoulders until the front legs hung over his arms and the back legs hung down by his feet. The head poked out stiffly in front of him, the big ears spread wide.

"Like this," he said, and started off, bent over and moving slowly upwind like a feeding caribou.

Kanguq mimicked the movements of the dwarf and was soon astonished to find himself within a dog team's length of the nearest animal. Then the dwarf slowly led Kanguq into the very center of the herd, and none of the animals seemed to notice them.

Kanguq saw that caribou were all around. They were so close that he could almost touch them. A bull caribou with a huge rack of antlers suddenly raised his head and snorted loudly, having smelled something. Kanguq stiffened in his tracks. But the dwarf moved on, imitating a feeding caribou, and the big bull soon settled down to feed again right beside Kanguq. The dwarf under the hide glanced slyly at Kanguq and smiled. Kanguq knew that he must decide what to do next.

Slowly, very slowly, he reached down and drew the long knife from its sheath in his boot top, and with a short, powerful movement, he drove it into the bull caribou's chest. The animal gave a great leap that tore the knife from Kanguq's hand, stumbled a few paces, and then with a sigh sank to its knees. The spirit rushed out of it, and it was dead. The other caribou looked at it for a moment, but believing that it was resting, they continued to graze.

The dwarf walked on among the animals, imitating their movements perfectly. He seemed not to notice that Kanguq had killed a

caribou. Kanguq watched him carefully, wondering what Taliqjuaq would do next, wondering also what he himself should do.

Suddenly the dwarf threw off his caribou-skin cover and stood upright, a man among the animals. Their antlers flashed upwards as they saw him for the first time. They snorted with alarm and bounded away, scattering in different directions. Their great splayed hoofs carried them swiftly across the snow, but soon they banded together, once more drawn by their instincts as a herd. In a few moments they were almost out of sight, leaving behind them a whirling cloud of snow crystals. All, that is, save Kanguq's dead caribou and two others who stood motionless.

"Start walking behind that one," called the dwarf to Kanguq. "Move toward our camp. Keep it before you. We can come back for your dead caribou tomorrow with the dogs and sled to haul it in."

The two caribou moved slowly in front of them as though dazed, and Kanguq realized that the dwarf had stabbed them both so quickly that he had not seen the motion. Taliqjuaq had stabbed them lightly in a special place behind the chest so that they could still walk. In this way the two hunters easily guided the caribou back to the snowhouse. One fell within a dog team's length of the igloo; the other dropped over right at the entrance.

"That is how to stalk and kill an animal," cried the old man, who stood beside the snowhouse watching them drive the caribou home. He held himself stiffly upright, supported by the big bow, and his old eyes glowed with pride as he thought of the boy becoming a man. With excitement he called to the old woman, asking her to come and help them with the skinning. He warned the dogs away from the caribou with a harsh command.

The next day Kanguq went out with the sled to bring in his caribou, but a starving wolf had found it in the night, and he brought back less than half the meat.

Slowly as the days passed, the air became warmer, and in the early mornings they heard the short, shrill mating call of the white-feathered ptarmigan. Bare patches of tundra started to show through the snow. The old man was slowly carving a piece of antler into the likeness of a caribou. This carving he rubbed and polished carefully, for he believed that such a friendly act would cause the caribou to wish to give themselves to the hunters.

Because the spirit of the hunt was still strong in him, the old man sometimes took Kiggavik and, using it like a staff, wandered slowly up the river hoping to find game. One evening, Kanguq met Ittuq, and they rested together before making their way back to the camp. The old man told Kanguq of a great journey northward to the Land Behind the Sun he had taken when he had been young and strong and his eyes could see great distances. Throwing back his head, Ittuq drew in a deep breath and in a rich voice sang a song about the musk ox and about the joy he had had in that far-off place:

"Ayii, Ayii, Ayii, Ayii,
Wondering I saw them,
Great black beasts,
Running, standing,
Eating flowers on the high plain.
On my belly I crept to them
With my bow and arrows in my mouth.
The big one reared up in surprise
As my arrow quivered in his chest.
The herd scattered
Running on the high plain,
And small I sat singing
By the big bull's side.
Ayii, Ayii."

The old woman was always busy and full of singing as she mended their clothes, dried their boots, and scraped the new skins.

One day she told Kanguq that she had placed some round black stones on the ice of a lake half a day's journey from their camp. Now she wanted to go and see if the sun had heated them enough to drop them through the thick lake ice and make holes for fishing.

Together they walked out across the land, and with every step they responded to the wonder of the quick Arctic spring as it burst around them. They could hear the water running in streams beneath the snow. So well did Kanguq and the old woman understand each other that they did not often feel the need to speak.

Reaching the lake, they both stopped, sensing something strange. Then Kanguq saw it. It was a pure black *qasigiaq,* a rare freshwater seal, lying out on the ice near the opposite shore.

"A beautiful skin," said the old woman softly. "That skin could make the best pair of boots in the land. Hurry, boy, before it sees you and dives down into its hole in the ice. *Qasigiat* are very easily disturbed."

Scarcely moving, Kanguq drew his bow from its case and carefully fitted an arrow to the bowstring. He paused, looking at the ground, thinking only of the black seal. Then with a smooth, even swing, he raised the bow and sent the deadly arrow winging along its course, straight into the animal's heart. The seal scarcely moved as its soul rushed out of its body.

"It was a long way to that seal. I see now that you will become a great archer," said the old woman with joy in her voice as they started out across the ice. Swiftly and cleverly she removed the richly spotted skin from the seal with her sharp moon-faced woman's knife. Cutting away the thick layer of white fat, she exposed the dark red meat underneath.

"When I was very young," she said, "and it was spring, I once came walking here with my grandmother to fish. Six days we stayed, yet she carried no food, no tent, no snow knife, only a little bone hook and fishing line hidden in her hood. When evening came, we lay down near a stone for protection and slept out under the open sky. My grandmother was a strong woman, full of ancient songs. She would put me on her back when I was a child and walk all day to catch one fish. Come now, we must eat meat, for meat in a human is like oil in a lamp. It gives one strength and heat from within."

After they had eaten their fill, Kanguq lay down on a high piece of dry tundra with the snow around him and watched the stars come out and grow bright as the sky darkened, and he thought again, as he often did, that there would be no real peace or joy for him till he had avenged the death of his parents.

The next morning he awoke and saw the sun was high, shedding its warmth over the land. There were bird sounds all around him. The old woman was already down at the new fishing holes made in the ice by the stones. She was fishing diligently with her small hook and hand line. Three fat red trout lay beside her.

Later, when they returned to the camp, the old woman scraped the remaining fat from the sealskin very carefully with her moon-shaped knife and soaked it in urine to remove all grease and to bleach the skin. Then she washed it many times in snow water and stretched it on a frame. The sharp night cold and the long sunlight glaring off the snow soon turned the skin sparkling white. Then the old woman cut the beautiful hide into careful patterns. She drew the finest bone needle from her little ivory case, and, using the thinnest, strongest sinew, she soaked and shaped and sewed a pure white pair of knee-length boots. She did not give these boots to Kanguq but hid them in her loonskin bag.

When the roof of the snowhouse collapsed on them from the heat of the spring sun, they all laughed with pleasure, for it was a sign that the geese would soon return and the fish would run once more in the open rivers. The old woman took many caribou skins and sewed them into a tent. Taliqjuaq cut the heavy sealskin thongs that held the long sled together, and using the runners to serve as tent poles, he covered them with the skins. This became their new summer home.

For two brief moons before the cold returned, millions of tiny insects swarmed in the clear, still air. The geese arrived in vast numbers to build their nests and to lay their eggs in the safety of the still marshlands where no man's foot had ever trod. Kanguq and Taliqjuaq hunted and fished throughout the short summer.

But soon the tundra turned red with the coming of early autumn. Each morning new ice formed on every pond, and the winds carried within them the hidden whips of winter. The caribou were on the move again, trekking southward toward the Land of Little Sticks, their big antlers shining, their light autumn coats sleek and perfect for making warm clothing.

Early one morning when the air was sharp and the sky filled with heavy clouds, Kanguq looked out of the tent and saw the old woman crouching alert and motionless on the far bank of the stream. Taking his bow and arrows, he hurried cautiously to the place where she waited for him. She nodded her head, and looking in that direction, he saw hundreds of caribou pouring along the bank of the river in single file, pawing the ground with their sharp hoofs and feeding. The young males threatened each other, raising their heads, shaking their great antlers, stepping stiffly sideways like graceful dancers.

Kanguq strung his bow slowly so he would not frighten the animals and notched an arrow against the string. He aimed carefully at a plump bull caribou, its sides bulging from the rich summer feeding.

"Wait," whispered the old woman. "Look at that beautiful one. Take that one," she urged.

He moved his bow until his line of sight seemed to reach out and touch the caribou with the light gray back and fine snow-white flanks. He released the arrow, and it silently flew straight to its mark. The animal reared up, ran out of the herd, and fell.

As he raised his bow again, the old woman called to him, "Quickly now, the one with the tan back and white belly."

Seeing it, he drove the arrow from his eye straight into its heart.

Three more she selected because of their whiteness, and three more he killed. Then the herd grew nervous, sensing danger, though they could not see or smell or hear it, and plunging through the shallow river, the caribou ran across the open plain. Swiftly they went, and so well did they blend with the autumn tundra that in a few moments they disappeared from view.

As they approached the place where the dead caribou lay, the old woman cried out with delight at the sight of such beautiful skins. Kanguq helped her as they skillfully cut and stripped the soft hides from the animals.

"Taliqjuaq will bring the dogs to pack home the meat," she said, and rolling up the precious hides, she tied them and flung them onto her back. In her mind she was already planning the scraping, stretching, drying, cutting, and sewing of the new skins. She hummed a song as they returned to the tent. In each hand, Kanguq carried a steaming red caribou liver as gifts for Taliqjuaq and the old man.

Later that autumn, after a blizzard, when the wind had packed great drifts in the river valley, they built a new snowhouse, the first

one of that winter. Taking down the tent poles, they lashed them together with crosspieces and remade their sled. Both the men and dogs felt the joy and excitement of the new winter with its sharp, invigorating cold. The open space of land and frozen sea became theirs once more to travel upon freely wherever they wished, and during the midwinter moon they decided to leave this inland hunting ground and return to the island.

They broke in the side of their snowhouse, fearing that evil spirits might lurk there and harm some other traveler. Then, like true nomads, they harnessed their dogs and drifted across the white expanse like leaves blown on the autumn wind.

When they reached the coast again, it was deadly cold, as the wind whipped in from the freezing sea, chilling a man until his bones trembled. In the second moon of winter, the long ice bridge formed and grew thick, and one early morning in the inky darkness they started to cross it. Before long, a storm blew in and the wind howled. The ice bridge heaved and cracked like a giant dog whip, but it held together, and by noon the next day they were safe in the shelter of the island's southern shore. Exhausted, they climbed up the steep passage, helping the old man, who could scarcely walk after their long, cold journey. When they entered the little stone house, the old woman lighted her lamp once more. It soon warmed the room and cast a soft glow among the bone rafters.

"It is good to travel far and to see each new day dawn over strange lands, for without moving we would not know the joy of returning home," she said, and the old man and Kanguq nodded their heads in agreement. For the first time Kanguq realized that he now thought of this island, Tujjaq, as his home, even though the painful dreams of his first home and lost family disturbed his sleep and caused his face sometimes to burn with anger.

On the following day, when Kanguq first saw Lau and her family of dogs running together, he was afraid. Nine of them there were now, big and white and swift as young falcons. When he climbed the island's eastern slope, the wolf dogs raced straight at him. Then Kanguq recognized Lau, who leaped and bounded around him, licking his hands. Two of her children snarled at him, but Lau warned them off with a growl. Although they were almost as large and strong as she, they obeyed her.

After the excitement of meeting again, Kanguq looked at the half wolves, half dogs, all of which he had last seen as pups. They all had thick pure white coats, long heads, and the pale, frightening eyes of a wolf. Their legs were longer than their mother's, and the pads of their feet were wider, perfect for running on soft snow. Although no man had fed them during the year, they were strong and healthy, for they had learned to hunt for themselves. During the summer when game on the island was scarce, he knew they

would have learned to stand belly-deep beyond the shore to snatch small fish from the water.

Kanguq noticed one of them, lean and handsome, more wolf-like than the others, who lay like a white prince beside Lau. Its strange eyes were more piercing than the rest.

"Amaruq," called Kanguq, and the animal, answering to the name of wolf, leaped up and came quickly to the place where Kanguq stood.

"You shall be the leader," said Kanguq. But he did not touch the animal, for as it stood silently before him, he sensed the quick strength and wild fierceness that lay hidden in the white wolf dog.

All through the next spring, Kanguq hunted seals and walrus that basked in the sunshine far out on the frozen sea. While hunting, he carefully trained the wolf dogs to work as a team, to obey his every command until they moved swiftly and quietly together during the hunt.

One day Taliqjuaq said to Kanguq, "They are not wide-chested and strong like the best sled dogs that can pull great loads of meat, but they have long legs and can run like the wind. They do not

fight much with each other, and they hunt for themselves. I have never seen such a team."

When Kanguq fed them rich walrus meat, the wolf dogs grew stronger and heavier, their chests widened, and their legs grew strong from pulling. All summer Kanguq hunted food for the island camp. He practiced shooting from every angle with his bow. Taliqjuaq helped him make a long knife with a curved antler handle that he shaped and bound until it fitted his hand exactly. This he sharpened, stone blade against stone, until its edge was as sharp as a snow owl's claw.

One day they found a bleached driftwood log that had been washed up on the island shore by the tide. Taliqjuaq and Kanguq split it by carefully driving sharp stone wedges along its center until it fell in two. Then they chipped these with short axes until the two pieces were shaped like long sled runners. These they left in the sun until they bleached bone-white. They made holes with a bow drill along the top of the wooden runners, and with seal thongs they lashed on other narrow slabs of driftwood for crosspieces to hold the sled together.

The autumn came again, and Kanguq knew that he was growing up. He was much stronger now, with great muscles in his arms and back from drawing the bow. He could heave his sled through the rough ice with ease. He often helped the powerful dwarf pull huge sides of walrus meat up from the sea to the place where they covered it with heavy stones to protect it from their dogs and wild animals. He felt glad to be alive and safe on their island home, and he thought of the old man and woman and the dwarf Taliqjuaq as his family. But deep inside him the restless hatred and the terrible desire to avenge his real family remained like a core of hard ice.

Kanguq was determined to tell the old man of the anger that burned within him, twisting his thoughts in the light of day and haunting his dreams at night.

One day Kanguq saw the old man alone on the rust-colored moss some distance from the little house and thought that now was the time to speak with him. He noticed how bent with age the old man had become as he stood blinking blindly in the autumn sunlight. He seemed to be listening—listening to something far away.

"Taliqjuaq, Taliqjuaq," the old man called to the dwarf. "Bring me my bow. Bring Kiggavik quickly."

Out of the cave came the dwarf, hobbling past Kanguq as he unwrapped the soft caribou skin that protected Kiggavik. One black arrow he carried, clenched between his teeth.

The old man took the great bow in his right hand like a staff, and thrusting it strongly downward, he snapped the bowstring into the upper notch. The dwarf handed him the arrow and moved away a few paces and crouched down. The old man dropped slowly, painfully, onto his knees, lifting his old face upward to the sky. His long white hair shifted about his shoulders in the light breeze, and his old eyes seemed weak and pale as mist.

Then Kanguq heard the first sounds high and far away. It was the calling of the geese. Snow geese they were, sending their wild music down to the earth as they winged southward from their summer nesting grounds. The very sound of them sent shivers up and down his spine.

Kanguq could now see them flying in a high white wedge against the blue sky.

"Kanguq! Kanguq! Kanguq!" called the geese, for the name the Inuit had given them was the sound of their call and their name also. Kanguq himself had been named for them.

The white geese were soon almost overhead, flying so high that they looked like drifting flakes of snow.

Kanguq watched the old man kneeling motionless, lost in thought. Then Ittuq slowly placed the dark arrow across Kiggavik and carefully notched it in the sinew bowstring. With one powerful movement he raised Kiggavik upward, drawing the great bow back as far as it would go. Smoothly he released the sinew, and with a mighty twang the arrow screamed into the sky.

Peering upward, Kanguq shaded his eyes and waited. Then, high in the blue he saw the great white goose, the leader, at the very point of the wedge, stagger in its flight and start to fall. At first it turned over several times as its great white wings, out of control, were caught by the currents of air. Then it plunged straight downward, falling, falling. It struck the ground before them with a tremendous thud, its dead weight snapping the black arrow in half.

The dwarf crossed the opening and picked up the big bird. He brought it to the old man, who remained kneeling on the ground, holding the great bow, Kiggavik, curved in his hands like the swift dark wings of a falcon.

"These are feathers for a white archer. It is right that you should have them. But you must never kill this bird nor eat its flesh, for you bear its name. You came to us from the wild geese, and when you die, your spirit will fly free and live with the snow geese once more. They are a part of you."

Kanguq took the wild goose gently in his hands. It was soft and warm and heavy, and the beautiful head on the slender neck curved back until it almost touched the ground. The powerful wing feathers lay open in death, white as wave tops, curved one against the other like wind-carved drifts of snow.

Kanguq wished to speak with the old man, but the right time never seemed to come. Ittuq was now almost completely blind, and much of the time he sat nodding back and forth lost in thought. It was as though his body remained with them and his mind went away, traveling in the distant lands of his youth.

One night when the old man was asleep, Kanguq quietly told the old woman of his troubled thoughts and that he must go and search the inland for the attackers who had destroyed his family. The memory of that terrible night burned within him like fire and would not let him rest.

The old woman stopped sewing and nodded sadly.

"Yes," she said, looking at her sleeping husband. "He told me four years ago that you would remain until the ice bridge formed this winter and that you would then go forth, driven by your desire to avenge your family. That time has now come, but I must say to you that hatred and revenge follow each other like two strong men piling heavy stones one upon the other until the stones fall, killing both men and perhaps many others."

Kanguq heard her words but did not try to understand their meaning, so crowded was his mind with the wild spirit of vengeance. Over and over again he planned the journey in his

mind, for he knew that he must go. He must be ready when the ice bridge formed during the midwinter moon.

Silently the dwarf helped him make new arrows, long and straight, with points as sharply ground as a weasel's tooth. To these arrows they carefully bound the feathers freshly plucked from the wings of the wild snow goose. Sadly the old woman made eight strong white sealskin harnesses for the team.

Kanguq ran the white wolf dogs every day and heaved the long sled until he, the driver, and his team grew wise and strong as they worked together. When he called to the leader, Amaruq, to stop or go, lead right or left, the wolf dog obeyed instantly and the team followed willingly.

One biting cold morning at the end of the first winter moon, Kanguq climbed the high stone cliff that surrounded their little house. From Tugjak's highest peak he looked toward the distant mainland and saw that the long ice bridge had formed. He hurried down and told the old couple that if the weather remained good, he would leave the following day.

When he awoke the next morning, a new fur parka with a full hood and new knee-length fur pants lay beside him on the bed. They were cut and finely sewn from the flanks of the caribou he had hunted on the inland plain. He had never seen anything so beautiful. He pulled these over his light inner parka and pants and found that they fit perfectly. The outer parka and pants were white as snow, and the wolf-trimmed hood rested warmly around his neck. He then put on two pairs of thick, warm fur stockings, knee high, and over these he drew the snug-fitting white sealskin boots.

The old woman, who had made the pure white clothing for him, was still sitting by her lamp. She smiled at him in a sad way and handed him the last three items, a tight hat made of white weasel skins, a pair of white fur mitts with leather palms, and a small white bag of grease and ashes.

There were no words that Kanguq could find to say to the old woman, and as he thought of all her songs and the joys they had shared during their long walks over the summer tundra, he felt a great sadness rise up in him. Picking up his white bag, he turned and hurried out of the house, for he could not bring himself to look at her.

The old man stood beside the entrance. The dog Lau was close beside him. His old eyes seemed not to see Kanguq, but with fumbling hands he reached down and grasped the great bow, Kiggavik. He held it out before him.

"With this bow I give you all my strength and power, my gift to see and understand. Take it. Use it wisely. Take it quickly," he said as the tears ran out of his blind eyes.

Kanguq looked at the old man and at Kiggavik quivering like the wings of a dark falcon in the old man's hands. He laid his own white bow at the old man's feet and took the big bow gently. He tried to but could not speak. Slowly he turned and walked away down the long snow-filled path that led to the sea ice.

Taliqjuaq had harnessed the team of white wolf dogs down below the cliffs on the frozen sea. The dwarf did not look at Kanguq as he tightened the leather lashings on the sled. Spread over the sled was the dwarf's sleeping skin made from the great white bear he had killed.

"You need that bearskin for sleeping in the cave," said Kanguq, starting to take the huge skin off the sled.

"Leave it on," the dwarf commanded in a harsh, rough voice that Kanguq had not heard before. "It is yours, white archer. Now, go with strength. Fly with Kiggavik," he said, and gave a sharp warning command to the wolf dogs, who howled and strained in their harnesses, eager to start the journey.

"Ush! Ush!" Kanguq called to the lead dog, and as the sled headed forward, he jumped onto it.

When the team had settled into a steady running pace across the snow-covered ice, Kanguq turned to look back. He saw the little dwarf figure standing alone before the jagged rocks of the island, peering after the team with his sharp eyes. But Kanguq knew that the whiteness of his clothing and the white sled and team had caused him to disappear like magic into the great whiteness of the ice bridge.

The wolf team traveled so fast that Kanguq dared not run beside the sled to keep warm for fear he might fall behind. He grew cold and would have frozen on the wind-whipped sled had it not been for his new and perfect-fitting clothing. The deep fur-trimmed hood protected his face from the stinging cold, and almost before he knew it, the team had carried him safely across the ice bridge. They reached the coast of the mainland before the winter moon had risen.

Kanguq halted the team with one sharp command and, walking forward, unharnessed the wolf dogs, calling each one by its name. From a rough skin bag on the sled, he shook out rich chunks of frozen seal meat that the hungry team devoured in an instant. Sitting quietly on the sled in the still cold, he watched the evening star rise above the coastal hills, while with his knife he shaved and ate thin delicious pieces of the frozen seal meat, the same food he had given to the team.

Kanguq then quickly built a small igloo, using his long ivory-bladed snow knife to cut and shape the blocks of wind-packed snow. He cut the blocks in a circle from below his feet and built the walls of the house around himself. Crawling out of the entrance after the blocks were in place, he filled the cracks with snow. Then he gently pushed Kiggavik and the skin of the great white bear into the igloo and crawled inside before fitting the snow-block door in place. He carefully pulled off his white outer parka and pants and rolled himself in his new sleeping skin that Taliqjuaq had given him.

Now he was truly alone, with a terrible task to perform. Lying there in the small igloo, he thought again of the dark night of the raiders and of his parents, lost to him forever, of his sister, Suluk, stolen from his sight. Terrible anger ran within him, and he lay shaking in the warm bearskin as though he were chilled to the bone. When the shaking passed, he drifted off to sleep and dreamed of lean, gaunt men with faces painted in wild designs.

The next morning he arose long before the light came into the eastern sky. He cut the igloo open with his knife and stepped out. In an instant the team was up, and he harnessed each dog. He placed Kiggavik carefully in its long protective quiver beside the separate pouch that held the arrows. He tucked it carefully between the soft folds of the white bearskin. This, along with the meat bag, he lashed to the long sled.

With a call to Amaruq, the lead dog, he set the dogs in motion. The whole team leaped forward and rushed southward, following the coast. He called commands to Amaruq, who led the team with a long, loping stride.

Two snowhouses he built and three days they traveled on the sea ice until they came to the barrier ice heaved up at the mouth of a great frozen river. Turning, they followed inland the broad path of snow-covered ice. Kanguq searched the snowy banks on either side, for it reminded him of his homeland as a child. But he could see no igloos, no sign of life in this lonely place, and the team carried him swiftly forward, following the river as it curved between the coastal hills.

The second night he stopped, fed the team, built his snowhouse, and, sitting on the sled, ate his only meal of the day. Kanguq watched the moon rise up like a giant's eye and cast its long light in a narrow shining path across the hills. He heard the river ice crack and groan in the still cold as though some monster lay hidden and strained to be released. Although Kanguq had never seen the little people, he knew that it was at a time like this a man could hear the river spirits laughing and the answering whistle of the shore spirits. He watched along the river carefully, for it had always been said that the little people of the spirit world loved to crawl out of a crack and lie upon their backs on the ice, kicking up their legs and chuckling in the very path of the moonlight. He thought perhaps he heard a small laughing sound, but in the pale light he saw nothing.

Then all was silent. The wolf dogs lay quietly around the snow-house, and Kanguq curled up in the warmth of his sleeping skin and slept until morning.

The third and fourth days' journey carried him far across the inland plain, and on the fifth day a great blizzard swept over the land. At first the air grew warm and huge flakes of snow whirled down. The wind whipped itself into a fury, and Kanguq could not see the dogs before him.

He stopped and built an igloo, though the wind was so violent that it tore some of the snow blocks from his hands. He fed the dogs the last scraps of seal meat and crawled into his igloo, where he slept and dreamed and waked and thought and slept again. For five days the winds thundered against his little house and tried to tear it from the land, but he had built it well and it stood firmly until the wind went moaning off across the plain, leaving only a vast white silence.

When at last Kanguq cut away the snow door and stepped outside, it was like a white magic place. The giants hidden in the wind had carved the snow into wild shapes, piling great drifts against the riverbanks. They had swept the lake ice clear of snow. Everything had changed, and the leaden-colored storm clouds hid the sun and stars and would not tell him east from west.

Kanguq bent down and with his bare hands felt beneath the snow, for under this new snow he knew that the old drifts ran north and south. When he moved his hands along the old hard ridges, he learned the direction that he must travel. Harnessing the team, he set out more slowly now. The dogs, like himself, were hungry from the five days' fasting.

They camped that evening on the edge of a low ridge that ran south as far as he could see. This ridge was what Kanguq had been looking for. From its height he could see any movement of men or animals crossing the plain.

On the following day they journeyed straight south along the ridge. Kanguq searched east and west but saw nothing until almost evening when, with a short command, he stopped the team. Far out beyond his right hand on the flat plain, he was aware of some movement. He watched and waited carefully. Then in the distance he made out a long line of caribou, looking like spots of silver on the horizon, slowly moving north. Kanguq was very hungry, the wolf team could not continue much longer without food, and he knew he might not see game again in this desolate country. But the flame of anger in him said, "Go on. *Go forward now.*"

He called a command to Amaruq, and the team pulled on until the waning moon rose again. Then Kanguq built another snowhouse and slept fitfully, for he was now weak with hunger.

When he stepped from his igloo in the morning, he saw a welcome sight. The wolf dogs lay before the entrance, their white coats stained with blood, and he knew in an instant that they had run silently as a free hunting pack in the night and had pulled down a caribou, fed themselves, and returned to him. There was a look of triumph in the green eyes of Amaruq and the others as they lay with full bellies licking their white coats clean.

For two days they traveled south, seeing nothing in the land save one snowy owl searching like themselves across the white expanse.

Late the following afternoon Kanguq saw in the distance the Land of Little Sticks. He had never seen it before. The small trees stood like gray ghosts silently listening on the plain. Beyond these first dwarfed trees, he could see there were larger ones and many more of them.

He camped early because he did not wish to sleep among the little sticks and because he feared that the dogs would tangle their long lines in the trees. Before he entered his new snowhouse, he looked around him in the twilight and listened carefully, and he knew fear inside himself. He was starving. He cut a piece of leather dog line and chewed it, hoping this would give him strength.

That night strange dreams whirled through his mind. When one of the wolf dogs gave a long, sad howl at the moon, he leaped up almost before he was awake and found himself crouched and ready, facing the entrance, his knife clutched in his hand.

He was out of the little house the next morning and had the wolf dogs harnessed before the moon grew pale. Before he had gone far, he saw the three stone men. These images must be the ones mentioned by the lean man from the River of Two Tongues. This surely was the place. Then he saw the sight that he had dreamed about for four long years, the frozen river that led into the Land of Little Sticks, and far away, almost on the southern horizon, thin columns of smoke rising in the still morning air. There were not ten fires, as the three men had seen long ago, but more than twenty.

He sat down on the sled, starving and alone. He remembered the terrible vision of his childhood, of the strong, lean men with bows and knives and clubs, of the big man lying with the arrows in his back.

But Kanguq started off again, driving the team cautiously toward the camp, following the river between the little sticks, and peering fearfully into every shadow. It was growing milder now, and the air was soft.

He halted the wolf dogs, and they lay down in the snow. He drew Kiggavik with its arrow quiver from beneath the lashings and turned the sled over to act as an anchor to hold the team. Then, slinging the bow and quiver across his back and checking that his long knife was safe in his boot, he started carefully forward. The soft snow, once he had left the banks of the river, was almost knee-deep.

He walked through the little sticks, guided by the thin columns of smoke rising before him, until he came to the top of a small hill. There spread before him was the First Nations camp where he guessed at least twenty families must live. Never, in his whole life, had he seen a place with so many people crowded together.

The shape of their tents was utterly strange to him. They were cones built of many long sticks with skins stretched tightly around them. White acid-smelling smoke rose from the opening at the top of every tent. Men he saw, and women and children, and many thin dogs. The men looked tall and dangerous, and there were many of them. He thought of himself, so young and yet planning to go alone against a huge camp of warriors. Again he felt the terrible pangs of hunger and fear, but deep inside himself he knew that he must act—and quickly before his strength failed him.

When it was dark, he slowly returned through the deep, heavy snow to the river and his team. He could not build an igloo, for the snow was too soft among the trees. Instead he rolled himself in the white bearskin and lay among his wolf dogs, hoping they would give him protection.

When he awoke, the land was covered with a light silver fog and big snowflakes drifted lazily down through the small trees. He rose and staggered off, dizzy from hunger as he once more left the dogs and made his way toward the dreaded camp. He remembered his father telling him that a starving man could live without food for a whole moon as long as he had snow to eat or water.

A sound behind made him whirl quickly and snatch at his knife before he saw that it was Amaruq who had worked free of the harness. The white lead dog stared at him with wise green eyes, and when Kanguq moved forward again, the animal followed silently in his footsteps.

Kanguq chose a different route this time because he wanted to go to a small frozen lake that he had seen near the camp. He stumbled occasionally in the strange foggy light that made all shadows disappear and distances difficult to judge.

Now Kanguq stood beside the snow-covered lake and looked across at the camp fires. He drew the white weasel cap from his parka hood and placed it on his head so that it covered his black hair. He pulled the small leather pouch from inside his parka and rubbed the mixture of white grease and ashes on his face and hands. Amaruq remained beside Kanguq, sniffing the strong smoky scent of the camp.

For a long time Kanguq stood stock-still out on the lake, looking up through the mists, searching for courage, while fearful visions

of Indians raced through his mind. Suddenly he shouted in a terrible voice, *"Dog people. Women killers. Kayak rippers. Igloo breakers. Come to me. Come to me now in the dear morning."*

He then howled like a wolf, and Amaruq joined him in a frightening chorus. Next he cried out like a loon laughing across a lonely lake. And last he roared like a bear fighting against many dogs.

There was a moment of silence in the Indian camp, followed by excited voices in a strange language that Kanguq could not understand. Among the trees he could see men running, bent forward like hunters fitting arrows into their bows as they rushed toward him. He screamed once more, like an angry falcon, and they all stopped and raised their bows.

Slowly he reached behind him and drew Kiggavik from his back. With his right hand he selected six white arrows from the quiver and stood them in the snow before him. A flight of Indian arrows struck around him. Some were very close.

He notched a seventh arrow in the bowstring and lowered his head in thought. Then he raised Kiggavik and aimed the sharp point straight into the heart of the nearest crouching warrior. But at that moment something strange happened to him.

A whirlwind of doubts rushed into his mind. If he harmed these people now, would they not wait and seek revenge again among his people? Would they not come yet again into the Inuit land, raiding and killing, carrying the old hatred forward from father to son to grandson? Was he not helping to pile hatred upon hatred like stones that might fall and kill everyone? Was he indeed any better in his quest for revenge than a mad dog that seeks only to bite and kill? Had the three starving men of his own kind not caused all this trouble long ago by raiding this First Nations camp and stealing meat?

A vision of the old woman's face seemed to drift before his eyes. Kanguq remembered all her gentleness and the wise things she had said to him. He moved the point of his arrow away from the man's heart. But his anger was not entirely spent. His eyes narrowed, and he clenched his teeth as he sent the arrow whistling into the heavy collar of the warrior's skin coat. It pierced through the fur collar and cut into his strange hat, pinning them together. The arrow then pressed so tightly across the warrior's throat that he screamed in terror.

Kanguq sent arrow after arrow whistling in among the warriors, ripping their clothing, terrifying them, but never killing them. Then they took aim but held back their second flight of arrows, for they could not see Kanguq disguised and hidden in his whiteness. He moved like a silver shadow disappearing in the mists and snow, and they cried out in fear.

They saw clearly the great bow Kiggavik, curved like a black falcon's wings, that rose and fell menacingly. Its bowstring sang. Its arrows flew against them, guided by the wild-goose feathers. The Indians were sure this was some winter spirit with a magic bow.

When Kanguq's arrows were almost spent, he heard a soft woman's voice among the rough strange shouting of the Indians. It called to him. It called to him in Inuktitut. It called his name.

"Kanguq. Kanguq. Brother of mine, I know your voice. I beg you, put down your bow. I am Suluk, your sister."

The warriors watched in terror. They did not know whether to stand or run as the Inuit girl, Suluk, walked out alone across the snowy lake to the place where the black bow hung poised in the air.

When Suluk stood before her brother, she rubbed her hand over her eyes, for she could scarcely see him.

"Brother of mine," she said, "are you a ghost? Or have you come to me after all these years when I have thought you dead?"

She reached out timidly and put her hand against his cheek to feel if he were real. Then she took his hand gently and began to lead him across the lake.

The warriors stood back as she led Kanguq through them into the very center of the camp. A hundred dark eyes stared out at them from the tents and snowy cover of the trees, watching the falcon bow, the great white wolf dog, and this faint ghostlike shadow of a man.

Amaruq stalked close beside Kanguq, his muscles tensed, ready to spring. A low growl rumbled steadily in his throat, and his green wolf eyes stared suspiciously around him, for he did not trust this place or these strange people.

Kanguq, like the wolf dog, was tense and uneasy. None of this was right. None of it was as he had planned it all these years. He had not taken revenge upon these people because of the vision of the old woman, and now, helpless and outnumbered among these warriors, he felt that they would surely kill him.

He eyed his sister walking beside him; her clothing was completely strange to him. It was made of caribou skin with all the

hair scraped away, and it had no hood. It hung evenly to her knees, where it ended in a long, dangling fringe. Her costume was painted with strange red and black border designs of a kind he had never seen. Below the skirt long caribou-skin leggings, fringed on the side, hung down to her moccasined feet. On her head she wore a round decorated cap, and her long hair was braided in an unfamiliar way. Strings of bright beads hung around her neck.

Kanguq tightened his grip on the long knife that was now concealed in the sleeve of his parka when a dark shadowy figure moved quickly from the shelter of the trees. It was an Indian who went and waited near the entrance of the tent that stood in their path. He was tall and lean, scarcely older than Kanguq, dressed in a costume not unlike Suluk's. Over his knee-length coat he wore a wide beaded belt and across his shoulder a wonderfully decorated game bag. His hat was shaped and pointed in a strange and handsome fashion. He stood still, full of dignity, like a hawk, alert and ready to strike. Kanguq noticed that he had removed the mitten from his right hand, and it hung tense and ready beside his long iron knife. His face was dark and handsome, but it seemed carved of stone and told Kanguq nothing.

Suluk spoke to the young man rapidly in a strange high-singing sound.

She then turned to Kanguq and said, "This is Natawa. He knows now that you are my brother." Then she went quickly into the tent.

The tall young man held back the skin flap that served as a cover for the entrance. Kanguq stepped over a long log and found

himself inside the dark interior. Amaruq lay down on guard outside.

Once inside, Kanguq waited until his eyes became accustomed to the dark. The tent was round inside, with the caribou-skin walls sloping upward to the blackened smoke hole in the center of the roof. Many caribou skins and some brightly colored blankets were piled against the sides of the tent for sleeping. A round flat drum made of stretched caribou skin hung by a long leather thong from the tent poles. In the very center, within a small circle of stones, Kanguq could see some glowing embers and the long log he had crossed at the entrance that was the main fuel for the fire. The log was never cut but merely pushed farther and farther into the flames. A large iron pot simmered over the fire.

Suluk led her brother to a special place by the fire and arranged the thickest skins for him to sit upon. The lean young man stepped inside the tent and squatted down across the fire from Kanguq. Much of his face was caught by the firelight, but his eyes were lost in shadow, and Kanguq could not read his face or guess what he was thinking. Kanguq saw the place where his arrow had torn open the skin of the Indian's garment at the throat.

"This man, Natawa, is my husband," said Suluk. "We have been married together since the first moon of summer."

Kanguq felt the cords of his neck thicken, for he could scarcely believe the words he heard.

Seeing the look on her brother's face, Suluk added quickly, "You must be hungry, brother of mine," and bent forward to stir the rich yellow broth that covered soft chunks of caribou meat.

Kanguq refused the meat and remained silent, watching the man carefully, ready for any sudden movement. He knew by the sound of Amaruq's low growl that the tent must now be surrounded by bowmen.

"For all these years," said Suluk, "I have feared that you and all my relatives were dead. When they first brought me here, I was always afraid. The children laughed at me and threw stones at me, and I was only used to carry water and skin out birds. But later I was adopted and had a mother and father. I learned to speak the language of these people, and all the children became my friends, and my new mother and father were always kind to me and taught me many things. Now I speak slowly and badly to you in our own tongue, brother of mine, because I have almost forgotten my own language.

"Sometimes in spring my soul cries out as I look across the barrens and remember how it used to be. I think again of times long ago when you and I made the long trek inland with our family. I remember the snow geese that laid their eggs on the soft tundra and the fat red and silver trout that drifted under the holes in the melting lake ice. I will never forget the night skies of the far north in summer when the sun walked on the hilltops and it never grew dark.

"But that is long passed now, like a dream. I am here among the little sticks with these people, and I think of them as my people. I wish that you could know Natawa as I know him and that he could know you as I know you. You and Natawa might have killed each other out there on the ice of the lake, and even now across the fire I see you each watching the knife hand of the other. I am only a foolish girl, but now I understand how wrong that is. I have love for both of you, and I have seen each of you dancing, singing, laughing, crying, and I know that, though you speak strange languages, you are truly brothers."

Then turning her gaze toward Natawa, Suluk said many words that Kanguq could not understand. Looking at her, Natawa's face softened, and he knelt forward and drew his iron knife from his belt. He drove it into the big pot and caught a great chunk of meat on its point. Turning the handle toward Kanguq, he offered him the knife and then lay back on the pile of soft skins.

Kanguq shook the long knife from his sleeve and pushed it aside. Then he placed the big bow, Kiggavik, behind him. His hunger returned to him in a rush, and as he smelled the rich meat, he remembered that he was starving. Not wishing to show his hunger, he ate slowly, savoring every bite until he was full.

Natawa stepped outside and spoke to the people who had waited there, and after he had spoken, the bowmen returned to their tents and Amaruq ceased to growl.

Almost all that night, Kanguq told them of his life after he had last seen his sister, and Suluk interpreted this to her husband.

When Kanguq had finished speaking, Natawa then told him of the time he had first seen Suluk when they were young, of their marriage and of the long adventure they had shared that autumn. They had paddled south in a canoe on a wide river with many white rapids whose banks were covered with tall trees. Natawa's white teeth flashed as he smiled and spoke of a country that seemed filled with wild animals of a kind that Kanguq had never seen. He spoke of black bears, of big red-headed birds that hammered the high branches like drummers, and great furry animals that climbed in the trees. He said these creatures had spotted coats, yellow eyes, and the long sharp claws of an eagle.

Toward morning they lay down on the soft furs, covered themselves with colored blankets, and slept together. When they awoke, Kanguq gave a start, for he could not remember at first where he was.

Suluk rose first and pushed the long log farther into the embers of the fire so that it started to blaze briskly, and she placed the meat pot closer to the flames.

Natawa spoke to her for a long time, and when he was finished, she turned and said to Kanguq, "He asks you to stay with us, to stay among his people. He asks you to join him in forgiving old wrongs, to hunt together with him, to fish with us when we travel to the high falls on the Singing River when it is springtime again, and to live together like brothers. Oh, will you, Kanguq? Will you do as he asks?"

"Tell him that I understand the things that you have said for him, that I would like to hunt with him and learn to speak with him, and that I am sorry about the arrow that came so close to his throat. I am horrified by the thought that yesterday I had it in my mind to kill him.

"I must return to the island, for the old people have become my family and I must help them. When I have seen that they are well and have food enough, I shall return to meet you at the high falls in the spring."

Together they left the tent and walked out through the camp.

Big flakes of soft snow drifted down through the dark trees, catching on and clinging to the branches and to the sides of the smoke-stained tents. Before each of these dwellings hung rich beaver and otter pelts stretched on sapling frames to dry. Suluk had told Kanguq the night before that the First Nations people prized these furs as trimming for their clothing. It was also their custom, she had said, to trade fur with strangers farther south for iron knives, pots, beads, and blankets.

As Kanguq walked, small children, as motionless as frightened rabbits, peered out at him from the tents. They watched carefully, for he was almost invisible in his white fur clothing against the snowy background. Behind Kanguq strode the yellow-eyed wolf dog.

When they came to a grove of trees, Natawa pulled delicately laced snowshoes from his back, slipped his moccasined feet into their bindings, and stepped off the trodden path. He traveled easily, with a swinging gait, over the top of the soft new snow until he arrived at the place where heavy haunches of caribou hung from the trees. Reaching up, he pulled four of these down and loaded them onto a toboggan that stood nearby. Throwing the line over his shoulders, he hauled the toboggan to the path, and with Suluk's help he followed Kanguq across the lake and through the little sticks until they came to the place where Kanguq's team waited patiently.

After the white wolf dogs were fed, Kanguq gave a short command, and they leaped into position, ready to go, waiting for the second command.

Kanguq looked into his sister's face and then at Natawa, who stared back at him, dark eyes narrowed as if in pain. Natawa said one short sentence to Suluk and was silent.

Suluk said, "He asks me if I wish to go with you. He says that he will hide his eyes if I wish to go with you."

One word she replied to Natawa.

Then to Kanguq she said, "I will always stay with him. But come as he asks in spring and fish with us at the high falls between the two lands."

Kanguq turned and faced Natawa, and in the ancient way of his people, he dropped his mitts on the snow and pushed back the sleeves of his parka to the elbow, showing that he concealed no weapons against the man before him. Natawa, understanding this gesture, drew back his own sleeves and stepped forward. Their fingers touched briefly, and without any spoken words they understood each other.

Kanguq called out to the dogs. They lunged forward and rushed out of the Land of Little Sticks toward the open wind-swept tundra. He looked back once and saw his sister, Suluk, standing silently beside her husband. A warm feeling spread through his body as he thought of her, alive and happy. All his anger was gone from him, gone, he hoped, forever.

Then the sharp sting of cold struck him, and he laughed aloud with pleasure. He was returning to his own land. He would travel to the island of Tujjaq and talk with the old man again. Ittuq was a great teacher and had taught him many things about archery and about life. The old woman had tempered his feelings for revenge and had helped him to understand himself. They were his people.

Kanguq shouted with joy. Soon he would see the dwarf once more and hear the songs of the old woman. Suluk was safe. His wolf dogs ran fast. The great falcon bow, Kiggavik, was lashed safely to his sled. But, best of all, when the spring sun came and released the river at the high falls, he knew he would see his sister and Natawa.

A great happiness rose up in him, and suddenly the words of a song rushed into him from the sky, and knowing them, feeling them inside himself, he sang them boldly into the very teeth of the north wind. His ears, once hearing the words, would remember them forever:

> "Ayii, Ayii, Ayii, Ayii,
> I walked on the ice of the sea
> And wondering I heard
> The song of the sea,
> The great sighing of new-formed ice.
> Go then, go, strength of soul,
> Bring health to the place of feasting.
> Ayii, Ayii."

AKAVAK

Akavak awoke slowly, feeling the soft warmth of the caribou-skin robes against his naked body.

He listened but could not hear the wind giants that had tried to bury the snowhouse for days. Yes, they were gone now. Everything was deadly silent.

He lay in the midst of all his family on their wide skin-covered bed of snow in the igloo of his father. The big seal-oil lamp that gave light and heat to their house was almost out.

Akavak watched his breath rise slowly like steam toward the domed ceiling, then freeze into small white crystals and fall onto the dark furs that spread across the bed.

In the darkness, Akavak heard his grandfather sit up, unroll the parka he had used for a pillow, and draw it slowly over his head. He heard him lean forward, puffing heavily as he pulled on his dogskin pants and his knee-high sealskin boots. Then the old man slid out from between the warm furs and heaved himself down off the wide sleeping platform. Bending low, he made his way along the narrow snow passage that twisted through the meat porch and upward to the entrance.

When his grandfather stepped outside of the snowhouse, he coughed harshly as he breathed in the sharp, searing cold of the morning air. Then Akavak heard him whistle three times and knew he must be calling to the night spirits that fling their weird, glowing patterns among the stars. This whistling surely meant that he could see the northern lights and that at last the wind giants had swept the whole sky clear.

As the old man moved away from the entrance of the igloo, Akavak heard the snow squealing in pain beneath his feet. It must be very cold.

Akavak looked toward his father, now awake, supporting his weight on one elbow. His dark eyes sparkled, and his strong white teeth flashed in the half dark as they reflected the flickering light of the stone lamp.

"Your grandfather must see his brother before he dies," said Akavak's father. "Long ago he promised to do this. Now he grows old, and there is only a little time. You are the one who must help him.

"His brother's land we call the Kuujjuaq. It lies to the north. There a mighty river flows into the sea. I have never seen that place, but it is said that great herds of walrus come to the very edge of the ice. In summer countless birds lay their eggs on the cliffs. When the moon is full in spring and again in autumn, the whole river is alive with fish.

"The way to that good land is long and hard. You must avoid the high mountains that stretch inland. Stay on the coast and travel on the sea ice. There are no people to help you on the way, for the huge tidal flats prevent hunting there during the time of open

water. It is a starving place between our last cache of food and the Kuujjuaq. There is a big fjord you must cross. Sometimes thin ice makes that impossible. If that is so, perhaps you should return here.

"I cannot take your grandfather there," Akavak's father added, "because we have not enough meat in our caches. In order to feed this family, I must hunt every day that the weather allows. So, this long journey falls to you. Go with him as he has asked and care for him, for his legs have grown stiff and often his eyes water in the wind until he cannot see. Sometimes when the day ends, you will see him tremble with the cold. But he will not complain. Then you must stop early and help him build a snowhouse.

"Remember that he is strong and determined and almost always wise. He knows the way to the land of his brother, for he traveled that way long ago when he was a young man. Listen to the words he says to you and learn from him, for that is the way in which all knowledge has come to this family. No man can build a better snowhouse, and when he commands that team of dogs, it will move for him as though it were his legs and arms, a part of himself.

"But sometimes now he does not hear the words that are spoken to him, and his eyes stare, and his spirit seems to go away from him and wander to some distant place, for he is very old. If he does not seem to hear you and his spirit appears to leave him, you must then be careful and decide everything for him.

"Take care of him and of yourself. Go with health and strength. That is what I have to say to you."

"Yes," answered Akavak, for it was the only word he could find to say to his father.

Akavak sat up quickly and drew on his warm fur parka and pants. This immense journey would take him into a new world, and he was secretly delighted. Until now he had never traveled more than two sleeps away from this place where he had been born fewer than fourteen winters before. Also, he had rarely seen a stranger.

Saimataq, his mother, was a wise and kindly woman. Silently she reached up to the drying rack beside her place on the bed and handed him warm caribou-skin stockings and new sealskin boots that she had finished making in the night.

With nervous wonder in her voice, she whispered to Akavak, "Last night while you were sleeping, your grandfather told us many things about his youth when he lived in the far-off land of his brother. I understand now why he wishes to return to that place. He gave us names to be used for children in this family that have not yet been born, for he was anxious to have me understand their importance. I believe that he does not expect to return here. What will become of you? I think of you both: one too young and one too old for such a journey. I am filled with fear."

She watched her son's handsome smooth-skinned face, his long blue-black hair, and the quick movements of his strong arms. She tried desperately to engrave his image on her mind forever, for she might never see her son alive again.

Akavak made his way out of the snowhouse and stood upright at the end of the entrance passage, feeling his nostrils pinch together in the burning cold. The trail would be hard and wind-swept, excellent for traveling. Around the four igloos of the camp, the snow stretched away white, then turned blue-gray, and finally disappeared in the night shadows that seemed to rise upward and blend with the star-filled sky.

Some of the sled dogs that had slept beneath the snow during the blizzard were sitting up now, still stiff with sleep. Their thick tails were curled tightly across their feet, and their backs were humped against the crackling cold. Akavak's grandfather had pulled down all the hunting gear and the coiled dog lines from their places on top of the snowhouse. He had his sealskin hunting bag slung across his shoulders. It contained all the things he needed to survive. His raised hood almost covered his long gray hair and the wide cheekbones of his wrinkled face. He was ready to travel.

Akavak's father followed him out of the igloo. Standing together, they watched the old man walking stiff-legged but fast across the hard-packed drifts. He headed toward the high meat cache. With the meat hook, he reached up and caught the skin bag of frozen walrus meat and jerked it down.

"He is leaving this morning—that much is sure," said Akavak's father. "Help him to load the meat on the sled and lash it tightly. It is enough to last you until you reach our cache at the big fjord. The dogs will run well with empty stomachs. Feed them when you camp tonight."

As dawn turned the sky gray-green in the east, Akavak heard the sea ice crack and moan as it was forced upward by the morning tide. A faint wind rose with the day, causing the fine snow to drift like smoke across the land. The wind ran its icy fingers beneath the warmth of Akavak's fur parka until he shuddered with the cold and was anxious to go, to be free, to run beside the dogs and make his body warm again.

When the sled was loaded and the dogs were hitched to their long lines, the old man stood before each person, looking straight into their eyes. Two of the neighboring women with babies on their backs opened their hoods so that the children might see him, perhaps for the last time.

"*Tavvauvusi ilunnasi.* Farewell to all of you," he called out in a strong voice.

He then turned away from the people of the four snowhouses who had gathered to see him depart. He started off alone on foot, using the chisel end of his slender seal harpoon to feel his way. Skillfully he chose the best path for the dog team among the jagged teeth of barrier ice that had been thrown up by the great tides. When he reached the smooth ice of the sea itself, he turned swiftly northward, holding himself upright, trying to look like a much younger man, for he knew that every eye in the village was upon him and he wished to leave them with a feeling of hope.

Akavak returned to the sled, after seeing that the six dogs were properly harnessed, and stood before the small group of men, women, and children. They were his family: his uncles, aunts, and cousins. The women hopped from one foot to the other trying to drive out the cold. They hummed soft songs and drew their fur hoods tight to keep the naked babies they carried from crying.

Akavak's father said, "At this time of the year, your grandfather's brother should be camped at the mouth of the giant river. Remain on the sea ice and follow the coast. That way you should not get lost. Beware of the mountains, son of mine." He paused, and then he said again, "Keep away from the mountains."

Then his father dealt Akavak a powerful blow on the side of the head, a thing he had never done before, for such a show of affection was never made to sons but was used only between full-grown men who were hunting companions or the best of friends. His father turned away, perhaps because he had shown his love so clearly, and walked quickly toward the igloos.

Akavak's mother and sister stood beside him, stock still, so gripped by fear that they could not feel the cold. His sister reached into her hood and drew out a new pair of fur mitts that she tucked under the lashings of the sled.

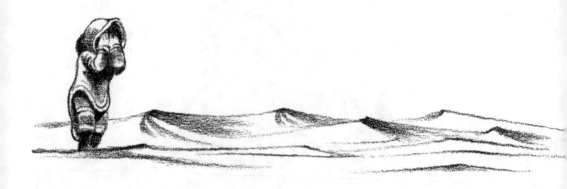

Akavak looked at her and smiled, remembering the good times they had had together. Then, without a word, he turned away, as was the custom of young men. Akavak drove his weight against the sled, and as it started to move, he called out to the dogs that whined and howled, eager for the trail, and they dashed forward. His sister and all the other children leaped onto the moving sled. The dogs followed the old man's path down through the sharp hummocks of the shore ice and out onto the hard flat snow that covered the frozen sea. Akavak's cousins laughed with delight at the speeding sled, as one by one they tumbled off, shouting, calling farewell to him.

His sister did not laugh. She was the last to leave the sled.

Akavak looked back and saw her standing alone in the flat whiteness, growing smaller as the distance increased. He raised his hand to her. So full of loneliness was she that she could not wave to him, and, turning, she walked slowly back to the village, her hands covering her face.

The team pulled together, running fast, quickly overtaking the old man. He watched them as they passed him—first the lead dog, a lean clever female named Naujaq. She would obey the driver quickly, going to the right or left at his command. Next came the big dog Pattiq. Strong as a bear he was, black, with wide shoulders and a deep chest for pulling heavy loads. Then came Kajuq, the fighter, gray and lean, with the long legs and the wicked eyes of a wolf. Following them, each hitched to the sled on a separate line, came the other three dogs, young, strong, and always hungry, still learning to pull within the team.

When the sled itself reached the old man, he ran to it and jumped on. He sat beside Akavak and placed his legs straight out before him. He pushed back his hood to cool himself and looked around.

Akavak watched him shading his old eyes from the light. At first he searched the flat level of the frozen sea and then looked inland, scanning the jagged white mountains that rose along the coast.

"Go there," said his grandfather, pointing to a place far before them where the mountains plunged into the sea and rose again as a rock-bound island. "We will pass through those narrows, and just beyond we will build our snowhouse for the night. Mark it well, for it will be dark by the time we reach that place."

At noon they stopped the sled and untangled the long dog lines. When they were ready to start again, Akavak drew one of the caribou sleeping skins across his grandfather's legs. The old man looked proudly away toward the narrows and did not seem to notice, but he did not remove the warm skin.

Akavak sometimes ran and sometimes rested on the sled, often calling encouragement to the dogs, guiding the course of the sled so that it was always pointed in the right direction.

It was fully night when they passed through the narrows and headed for the long, sloping shore. The moon was almost full and rode brightly among the stars. The snow sparkled all around them in its light.

The old man took up a bone wand, thin as an arrow and twice as long. With this he walked some distance, carefully probing into the hard, deep drifts. He seemed to be listening as he drove the point gently downward, feeling the texture of the snow. He walked further and probed again. Then he walked in a circle. Finally satisfied, he straightened up and called to Akavak, "Bring the snow knife."

With the long ivory knife, Akavak's grandfather first removed a large wedge of snow. Then he cut a big block, lifted it, and set it on the surface. He cut more blocks, placing them in a ring around himself. Then he started a second row spiraling upward.

Akavak chinked the outside of the blocks with fine snow, filling every crack. Although his grandfather worked slowly in the biting cold, he cut the blocks with great skill, and each one fit perfectly. He remained within the ring, building from inside, slowly walling himself out of Akavak's sight.

When the dome was completed, the old man cut a neat entrance in the base of the snow wall, and Akavak heard him beating the snow out of his clothing with the knife. Akavak pushed the stone traveling lamp and sleeping skins inside. Then he fed the dogs, watching them devour the chunks of frozen walrus meat. Satisfied, they curled on the new snow, their tails placed protectively over their noses.

When he crawled inside the igloo, dragging the bag of meat after him, Akavak found his grandfather holding a bow drill in his mouth, whirling it with his hands until the shavings in the wood socket smoked and burned. He lighted the wick in the seal-oil lamp, and the new snowhouse glowed in the reflected light. Akavak beat the snow out of his own clothing and the sleeping skins and unwrapped a packet containing choice pieces of seal meat. The meat was frozen hard, but when they sliced it thinly, it seemed to melt in their mouths. Akavak and his grandfather ate a good deal of it and drank quantities of ice water, for they were hungry, and, as was the custom, this was their only meal of the day.

When it was done, they lay back, side by side, wrapped in the warm furs. Just before he went to sleep, Akavak heard his grandfather laugh and say aloud, "I remember an old story about a tiny ground spider that one summer day crawled onto a boy's arm, and the boy drew back his hand to strike it. But the spider said to him in a thin voice, 'Don't kill me, or my grandchildren will be sad.' And the boy let him go, saying, 'Imagine, so small, and yet a grandfather.'"

They both laughed, and then Akavak's grandfather said, "A man grows old looking at the same hill behind his house. It feels good to travel once again."

They left the igloo at the first light of dawn, harnessed the dogs, and were traveling almost before Akavak was fully awake.

Six snowhouses they built and six nights they slept as they traveled northward along the frozen sea. Akavak wondered at the great mountains he saw for the first time and at the huge curling tongues of the glacier that reached down to the white sea. Each day was bitter cold, but they were glad, for the trail remained hard and the dogs ran swiftly, dragging the light sled with ease. They fed them well each night, for they knew that the cache that Akavak's father had made at the big fjord was full of rich walrus meat.

On the seventh day, they pressed forward at the old man's insistence until long after the moon had risen, and when they came to the edge of the big fjord, they could see the high stone cairn that marked the precious meat cache on the shore. By the light of the full moon, they also saw the tracks of a huge bear leading straight to it. Then, with horror, they discovered that the starving bear had ripped apart the rocks Akavak's father had so carefully set and frozen into place over the meat. The bear had devoured everything.

"It can't be helped," the old man said when he had examined the tracks. "The bear has gone far out on the sea ice many days ago. Already its paw marks are half filled with drifting snow. We could

never find that bear. We will sleep here tonight, and in the morning we will make our plan. We have lost food that would have allowed us to travel for half a moon, and we are left with nothing."

That night the dogs could only lick the stones of the empty meat cache and growl with anger at the smell of the bear.

When they crawled out of the snowhouse at dawn, the old man pointed across the misty flatness that stretched before them.

"That is the big fjord called Kingalik," he said. "It is a dangerous place at this time of the year. The strong tides force their way into the fjord and wear the ice thin, but with the hard snow covering, you cannot see many of the holes. Men have died here, and whole dog teams have been lost through the ice. We must cross it if we wish to reach my brother's land. Come now, I will show you the way."

They drove the team off the land and out onto the sea ice. Great clouds of white fog rose into the air. Akavak's grandfather waved his arm and called to Naujaq, heading the sled between the rolling banks of fog. Although they could not see any openings in the ice, they knew the holes were there since the fog was caused by open sea water striking the deadly cold of the Arctic air.

The old man called to the team, and the dogs halted instantly. He rose from the sled, and, taking the harpoon, he moved quickly forward, then stopped. Cautiously using the sharp bone chisel on the end of the harpoon, he jabbed through the thin snow surface to the ice below. Feeling that it was safe, he walked forward, and the dogs followed.

Before his grandfather had gone a dozen steps, Akavak saw the bone chisel break through the ice. Dark water flooded over the snow at the old man's feet. Moving as lightly as a white fox, the old man circled the weak place in the ice, for if he placed his foot upon it, he would surely have plunged into the freezing water.

He had not gone many steps farther when his chisel broke the ice again, and he quickly changed his course. The dogs followed him, crouching, their legs spread, fully aware of the danger. Akavak guided the sled and wondered at the path his grandfather set for them, for although the snow looked the same to him, his grandfather seemed to sense the bad places.

As they moved slowly forward, a wind blew in from the sea, causing the freezing fog to drift across the whole fjord, and they could no longer tell where the open places lay. Still the old man stiffly made his way onward, prodding the snow covering, turning this way and that, trying to find a path through the treacherous holes in the thin ice.

Then Akavak saw his grandfather suddenly fall flat on his back, his arms and legs outstretched. The ice had broken before him. His feet were in the water, but by falling, he had managed to spread his weight upon the thin ice. Quick as a weasel, he wriggled backward, away from the gaping black hole. Then he got onto his hands and knees and crawled cautiously until he could rise to his feet and walk back to the sled.

"We can go no farther," he said in a sad and weary voice. "The ice is too thin, too dangerous, and the fog blowing in makes it worse every moment. See, even now it hides our tracks back to the land."

Suddenly in the mistiness before them, they heard a strange snorting and blowing and a violent thrashing of water. The sound came to them again and again.

"What is that?" whispered Akavak, for he greatly feared this deadly place.

"*Allannguat!*" cried the old man. "Narwhal, great spotted beasts, four times the length of a man, with a long, thin ivory tusk thrusting out before them."

Straining their eyes, Akavak and his grandfather finally saw the narwhal through open patches in the heavy mists. Many of them were plunging upward, gasping for air at the breathing holes in the ice.

"Oh, how I long to drive my harpoon into one of those great beasts of the sea," cried his grandfather, his arms outspread with excitement. Yet he dared not move a step forward on this treacherous ice.

"There before you is all the meat we need for many winters, but we cannot have it. Tonight the whales will keep these holes open and leave when the tide changes. There is no help for it. We must go back."

They turned the team carefully. Akavak walked ahead, and the old man rode on the sled. They searched desperately for their earlier trail. As the fog thickened, Akavak had sometimes to feel in the snow for the old sled tracks, finding them in the darkness with his bare hands.

When at last they arrived back at the snowhouse they had left that morning, they went to bed tired, hungry, and full of despair.

When Akavak awoke, he saw that his grandfather had already left the igloo. Akavak dressed quickly and crawled outside. In the faint light of morning, his grandfather walked toward him holding four ptarmigan. Small white feathered birds they were, with furry feet and dark rich flesh. Carefully the old man threw one to Naujaq and one to Pattiq. Each dog caught the bird in its mouth and gulped it down, bones, feathers, and all, before the rest of the team could fight for it.

Inside the snowhouse, Akavak and his grandfather squatted on their heels and pulled the warm birds apart, devouring every scrap of blood and meat, sucking each bone clean. Finally they lined the insides of their boot bottoms with the softest feathers.

"We will travel up the big fjord," said the old man, "and see if we can find some other place to cross."

This they did, trying many times throughout that day and the following day to find a way over the treacherous ice. But they were always driven back.

On the third morning, they could see the end of the big fjord and a valley where a narrow frozen torrent twisted down from the mountains to the sea. As the sun rose, it lighted the steep red granite cliffs that stood on the opposite side of the fjord and revealed the rough tumble of ice that stretched beyond their view along the base of the cliffs.

"Even if we could cross the fjord at this place," said the old man, "we could not hope to climb those cliffs or travel through that rough ice along the opposite shore.

"There are only two things we can do. We can return home, or we can travel up that river valley you see before you and cross the high glacier into the mountains. Whatever we do, we must move quickly, for we have no food. Traveling to my brother's land from here is shorter than to return home."

"My father said that we should keep out of the mountains," answered Akavak boldly. "He said that we should beware of the mountains."

"Yes, yes," said his grandfather impatiently, "but your father does not know the mountains as I do. I traveled across this glacier before he was born. I know the way across the high plateau that leads to my brother's camp. I shall show you that trail. I long to move in the mountains again. Once we reach the plateau, we need only slide down the other side, and we will arrive in my brother's land.

"It is hard traveling in the mountains, but it is wonderful to see. Up there among the clouds, you can feel your back against the sky. Even the snow geese in summer fly far below you. Grandson of mine, would you like to go that way? Would you like to see the high place?"

"I don't know," said Akavak slowly. And he added, "My father said we should stay near the sea."

His grandfather did not seem to hear him.

"The weather is fine now, and we cannot wait longer," said the old man. "I am eager to end this journey.

"Musk ox, great black beasts of the high plain, live in the mountains, and we shall have them to eat and to feed our dogs. It is the only way."

What could Akavak say to such a wise and powerful man, the one who had taught his father? He could say no more. He could only help him to reach the far camp of his brother, or he would surely seem to be a coward, one who at the first hint of danger rushes back to his own snowhouse to hide among the women.

Looking straight at his grandfather, Akavak opened his eyes wide to show agreement.

His grandfather stood up stiffly, calling to the dogs, urging them toward the frozen river. The weather was cold and clear, and the sun was held in a huge silver ring of light. The snow on the mountaintops caught the light and shimmered like white clouds seen in summer.

In the paleness of evening, they reached the very end of the big fjord and stopped at the twisted river. It was solid, glaring ice. They unharnessed the team and built a snowhouse on the edge of the land.

That night Akavak had a strange feeling as he shoved the sleeping skins into their new igloo, for he did not like the great icy wall of rock that rose behind him. He had heard endless tales of Igtuk, the boomer, a dreaded mountain spirit who runs in the high places, and of the tuurngait, dwarf people who hide among the rocks. He was both excited and afraid, for the mountains seemed dangerously silent. His people were sea hunters, coastal people used to slim kayaks and the crushing ice of the sea but fearful of the high places and the terrible storms that raged there.

Akavak awoke once in the night and heard his grandfather call out in his sleep, shouting his brother's name again and again, and when he looked at the old man in the flickering light, he saw that his face was covered with sweat, although it was freezing cold in the snowhouse.

In the morning, with great care, they lashed their few possessions onto the sled and repaired the dog lines. Their path into the mountains would be a hard one.

From the first moment, their trail slanted upward. Akavak was never able to sit on the sled, and only at first could his grandfather ride. Akavak walked beside the sled, following along the river course, keeping the dogs away from the glare ice where they slipped and could not pull.

By noon, both Akavak and his grandfather were walking, and then pushing and shouting at the dogs, urging them forward. A big Arctic hare bounded away from them, but before Akavak could get the bow off the sled, a huge snowy owl swooped on silent wings over the team of dogs and, plunging downward, caught the hare. Still struggling, the feathered hunter and its prey disappeared from sight.

To his grandfather, Akavak said, "One has to be quick to stay alive in these mountains."

They camped that night at the bottom of a steep waterfall, frozen smooth and solid between two dark red walls of rock. The dogs moaned with weariness and with hunger.

"Is this the same path you took long ago?" Akavak asked his grandfather when they were wrapped in their sleeping skins.

"Yes, this is the river trail, and I remember these falls. It is a very difficult place."

In the first light of morning, Akavak's grandfather showed him some hand- and footholds in the ice and granite. Tying two long dog lines together, Akavak started the dangerous climb. Straight up the side of the frozen waterfall he went, until he was almost halfway. Then he slipped and fell back, arms outstretched. The dark rocks flashed past his eyes—then he landed in a deep bank of snow. All the wind was knocked out of him, and for some time he could not speak. As he started to test his arms and legs to see if they were broken, he saw his grandfather's worried face appear above him.

"Perhaps we should go back," said the old man, holding on to Akavak's arm. "Perhaps it is too hard. I cannot help you climb such a place."

As breath returned to Akavak, he remained on his back, staring up at the frozen waterfall, his eyes searching for the jagged footholds.

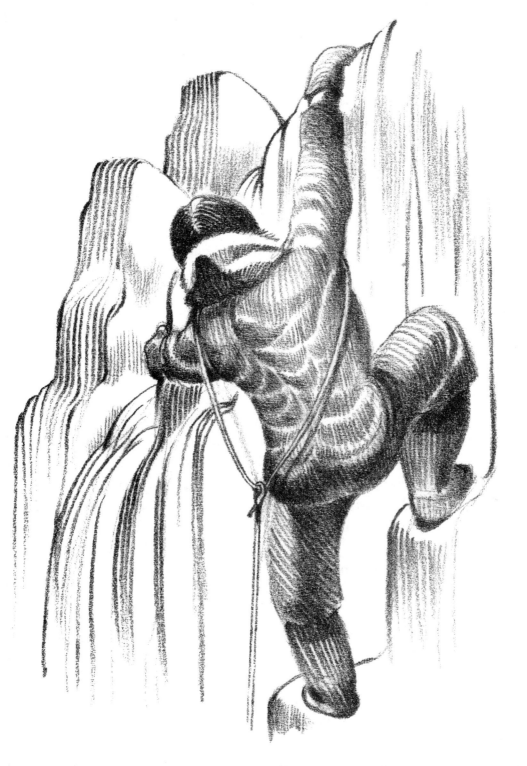

"I will go up. I will climb that place," he said with determination, for now, like his grandfather, he could feel the magnetic power of the mountains, and he did not wish to turn back.

With the long dog line tied around his waist, he climbed again. He moved more carefully this time, testing every handhold, pressing his body close to the hard ice. When at last he reached the top and drew himself onto the flat ledge, he lay there, gasping for breath until his strength returned to him.

Then he stood up, and the old man called out to him, "Good! You have made it. Find a strong foothold, and I shall tie Naujaq so that you can pull her up to the ledge."

The old man pushed the lead dog up as far as he could, and then Akavak hauled her the rest of the way, hand over hand. She whined and struggled to find footholds, scrambling against the icy rock face. When she came over the edge and Akavak untied her, she licked his hand.

Akavak lowered the rope again. His grandfather tied on Kajuq next, and Akavak attached the upper end of the line to Naujaq's harness. Together they hauled the big dog up the frozen falls. Working above and below, the grandfather tied each dog carefully, and Akavak and the team lifted each one to the ledge. Then the sled was stripped bare and raised, followed by the precious lamp wrapped in the sleeping robes.

It was almost dark when, with great care, Akavak, Naujaq, Pattiq, and Kajuq hauled the old man to the top.

For some time, Akavak and his grandfather squatted together in the darkness, so tired they could not move. They themselves had worked like dogs all day and were starving, and yet their last snowhouse lay directly below them. Akavak threw down a chunk of snow onto its roof and laughed without joy, because it did not seem possible that it could be so close.

Slowly they went about building a new snowhouse. It was deadly cold in the mountains, and they feared a sudden storm. Akavak's back that had been wet with sweat turned clammy cold, and his bones trembled.

"We will reach the top tomorrow," said the old man. "If the weather stays clear, we will reach the top before dark."

In the flickering light of the lamp, Akavak drew off his damp parka and lay in the dry warmth of the sleeping skins. He seemed to see his grandfather for the first time. A strong, proud old man he was, his face brown and hard and seamed like the rocks of the mountains. His hair was almost white and hung to his shoulders. But his eyes were the most important part of him. They were half hidden under deep slanting lids that protected them from the wind and glaring snow, but when the black pupils of his eyes flashed, they were like two spots of sunlight on dark water. Akavak could tell by his grandfather's face that he had seen many things, good and bad. When his grandfather was young and in his full strength, he was famous as a drum dancer and singer. His hunting companions said that he had once harpooned and held a walrus until it ceased to live, and then with mighty strength he had pulled it out of the water onto the ice by himself. No man among their people had ever done this before. But now his strength was almost gone, and his big square hands with the wide powerful thumbs trembled when he tried to light the lamp.

When Akavak left the snowhouse in the morning, he saw long,

thin white clouds flaring across the sky. These were driven by high winds far above them. His grandfather looked at them but said nothing. Akavak watched him hurrying to harness the tired, half-starving dogs.

They pushed forward once more, finding that the air was thin and hard to breathe. Akavak was so hungry that he sometimes lost all sense of time and seemed to float beside the sled.

He had been climbing in this trance for some while when he noticed that his grandfather was no longer beside the sled. Looking back down the trail, he saw him sitting hunched in the snow, his head on his knees.

Akavak halted the dogs and hurried back to help him.

"Go on. Go on," said the old man in a slow, thin voice. "I will rest here a while and then follow you to the top."

"No, Grandfather. You will come with me now. We must stay together," Akavak said with determination.

Akavak helped his grandfather up and supported him to the sled. Then he wrapped a caribou sleeping skin around his shoulders. The old man lay half on the sled but managed somehow to push with his feet, and in this way they started upward again. Akavak shouted at the dogs and beat on the wooden runners to frighten them, and they crept steadily forward.

Finally he could see the top, but he did not dare to rest in their slow passage upward, for the sky was darkening and clouds now hid the high peaks. The wind rushed in from the southwest, howling as it struck the frozen mountains.

Soon they were climbing the last rise, and then they suddenly

stopped and stared. The wide glacier lay before them, gray and ancient, laced with new white snow. Beyond it stretched the great flat plain of the high plateau, in places blown entirely clear by the violent winds, so that huge patches of tundra and many stones shaped like skulls were exposed to sight.

The dogs lay down, and the travelers turned the sled onto its side, against the rising wind. They, too, lay down, waiting for their strength to return to them.

"Come," said the grandfather. "We must cross the glacier there at the narrow place. Beyond it we will build a snowhouse."

Slowly they followed the dogs, stumbling across the blinding whiteness of the glacier. Once they heard it creak and moan beneath their feet.

"I do not like this place," said Akavak's grandfather, and he slid the harpoon out from under the sled's lashings. He started to walk forward, feeling carefully before him with the bone chisel. But for once his keen instinct for danger warned him too late.

With an awesome "swoosh," the snow around Akavak collapsed and fell into a great yawning blue abyss. He watched with horror as the scrambling, howling dogs disappeared. Then, as though by evil magic, the sled beside him slipped away, and he could no longer see his grandfather. In the swirling snow, Akavak's foot caught on something as he started to plunge into the awful abyss. Half turning, flailing, gripping, he lost his mitts and felt his bare hands strike something solid. It was the edge of the ice wall. He held on for his life. The thunder below him died away, and everything was silent again.

His muscles ached with deadly weariness, and his bare hands grew numb against the ice. But still he waited, his eyes closed, holding on to life with his fingertips. How long before he, too, must fall?

He did not see the rough old hand reach over the edge of the abyss, but he felt it grasp him by the hood of his parka, and another hand took his wrist. A rasping voice called, "Kajuq, Kajuq!" and in another moment he felt a sealskin line lashed around his wrist.

The old man called, "Ush, ush," to the dog. Then Akavak felt his hood jerk upward, and his arm was nearly pulled from its socket as he was drawn up out of the gaping hole in the glacier.

The boy and the old man lay beside the open crevasse, too exhausted to move. Kajuq, the starving dog that looked like a wolf, stood over them, with the dog line still attached to Akavak's wrist. For a moment it looked as though Kajuq was the hunter and these creatures stretched on the snow were his prey.

Akavak's hands were white and would not bend. His grandfather held them under his own parka, against the warmth of his body, until they burned like fire and the fingers could move once more. Then, because Akavak had no mitts, he drew his hands up into the long fur sleeves of his parka.

The sled and all the dogs were gone save Kajuq. Akavak could scarcely believe the swiftness of death that had taken Naujaq, Pattiq, and the others and buried them deep in the glacier forever.

The three staggered away from the awful blue hole and fearfully crossed the remaining tongue of the glacier. When they reached solid ground once more, they felt on their faces stinging grains of icy snow that blew down from the surrounding peaks. Slowly they made their way toward a small gully on the high plateau. It would give them some protection from the mighty force of the rising wind. They shambled on, the old man holding Kajuq's broken harness for support. Akavak tried not to think of what they would do now. They had no food. Without dogs or sled, there could be no going back or forward from this frightening place.

Akavak saw it first, half buried in the snow. It was so old and frozen that the dog did not even smell it. Two great horns curved upward, and one empty eye socket stared at them from the whitened skull.

"*Umingmakk,*" said his grandfather, "musk ox, long dead, killed by wolves perhaps."

"Nothing left," said Akavak sadly, kicking away the snow from the bare bones that lay scattered like gray driftwood among the useless tufts of long hair.

Bending over to examine it, the old man said, "That is a piece of skin, strong heavy skin," and he pried the end of a large stiff piece away from the frozen ground. Reaching into his hunting bag, he drew out a small knife and gave it to Akavak, together with one of his mitts.

"Cut away as large a piece as you can," he said. Then the old man stamped hard on the bleached skull, and the two big horns broke away.

"Bring these also," he said, and without another word he limped away toward the rocky cliff at the end of the little gully. In the wind, the caribou sleeping skin that was still wrapped around his hunched shoulders flapped like the wings of some ancient bird.

Akavak watched his grandfather as he edged along, carefully studying the cliff face, sometimes taking off his mitt to feel it. Then suddenly he dropped to his knees and started scraping and digging in a frenzied way. Akavak wondered if the time had come, as his father had warned, when his grandfather's spirit might wander away from him and he must take care of him.

With the knife, Akavak went on hacking and pulling at the useless frozen skin, looking at the gaping holes in it, knowing that it could have no warmth. With a jerk, he pulled free a large piece of the hide and straightened up.

He saw his grandfather walking slowly toward him. In his hands he held four stones. Wearily the old man chose a site and waved to Akavak to put the frozen hide down on the snow and place the stones on top. From his hunting bag, he drew a thin ivory blade and licked it until it was covered with a thin coating of ice and could be used to cut the heavy snow blocks. Together they worked and built a small strong igloo to stand against the forces of the mountain winds.

Once again, Akavak's grandfather cleaned the snow out of a hollow in the largest stone and, taking a small pouch from his hunting bag, removed some frozen seal fat. He held a piece of this in his mouth to soften it. Next he cut a small piece off his inner clothing to serve as a wick, and then he whirled his bow drill in its wooden socket until the dry wood shavings smoldered and burned. Carefully he lit the oil-soaked wick, and it sputtered and burst into flame, casting a small warm glow inside the sparkling white of the new snow walls.

They placed the frozen musk-ox skin on the soft snow floor, and over this they spread the caribou skin the old man had worn around his shoulders. They lay down with Kajuq between them, using the dog's body heat to keep them from freezing.

That night, the terrible wind screamed and thundered over their small igloo, trying to tear it from the high plateau and fling it down the mountains. But their house was strong and round and carefully trimmed, with no corners for the wind to grasp, and as Akavak drew his head deep into his hood and hugged his arms next to his body inside his parka, he thought, *I am alive, and my grandfather is alive, and together we shall cross this high plateau and see the land of my great uncle that lies beyond these mountains.* He said that to himself, again and again, until he drifted off to sleep. He dreamed of clever Naujaq, and Pattiq the strong one, and the three young dogs lost to him forever.

When Akavak awoke, he heard the sharp click of stone against stone. He rolled over and saw his grandfather hunched beside the light, holding a flat stone in his hand. His grandfather judged the

angle, then carefully struck the stone a sharp blow, causing a chip to fly off. Again and again he struck the flint, each time examining the shape. Gradually, as the day wore on, the stone was formed into a sharp blade, almost as long as Akavak's hand.

On the following day, the wind continued to thunder against the house. Akavak and his grandfather chewed pieces of skin cut from their boot tops to ease their terrible hunger, but always the old man went on grinding and sharpening the chipped blade.

They slept again, and so dark and terrible was the storm around their house that they could not tell if it was night or day.

When they awoke, Akavak's grandfather said, "When I slept, I dreamed." As he spoke, he trimmed the dying lamp wick and squinted his old eyes into the flame. "I dreamed that I walked up along the shining path of the moon and flew among the stars. I could see all the mountains and the rivers and the sea beneath me. Great herds of caribou I saw, and mighty whales rolling in the sea, and huge flights of geese. Seeing these things seemed to ease my hunger. I was pleased to have such a night journey, but when I grew tired, I found that I did not have the power to return to the earth. I felt a great sadness, for I knew I would not see my son or my grandson again, or my brother who lives beyond this mountain, or his sons. My mind was full of grief that I had not visited them. That was all that I minded about leaving this earth.

"And when I awoke just now, I thought again and again that I am an old man and may never reach my brother's land, and my hand shall not touch his hand again."

Akavak could not answer his grandfather, but he knew that what he said was very important to him.

With the new stone blade, the old man showed his grandson how to shape and polish the musk-ox horns. Akavak then scraped out the hollow insides until they were smooth. When they were finished, he filled the new cups with snow scraped from the inside walls of the igloo and held them above the lamp until the snow melted and turned to water. As Akavak held the cups over the flame of the lamp, he thought that although the great storm held them like prisoners in the little house, he and his grandfather were always busy when they were awake, working to stay alive. They were determined to leave the mountain.

They slept and woke again with pangs of hunger, listening grimly to the raging storm.

The frozen musk-ox hide was now soft and soggy, having partly thawed from the heat of their bodies. Akavak held one end while his grandfather poured melted snow water from the musk-ox horns over the skin. When it was soaked, his grandfather twisted and rolled it tightly into a staff as tall as Akavak, and with thin strips cut from the hide, they bound the limp staff along its whole length. When this work was done, they were both weak and tired and went to sleep.

Akavak and the old man awoke in the lonely time just before dawn. The dog Kajuq was snarling, drawing back his lips to show his big teeth. The hair on his neck bristled, and his yellow wolflike eyes glared at them wildly. Suddenly they both feared him, but although the old man held the stone blade ready, he did not want to kill the dog.

"Cut away the snow door," his grandfather said in a quiet voice.

Akavak quickly obeyed, and Kajuq rushed out into the dying breath of the storm, howling in his madness.

"I think he will not go far," said the old man, "for he needs us as much as we need him in this strange place.

"Take this rolled musk-ox hide outside. Mind that it is straight, for I may need to use it as a staff to help me down off this mountain." As he spoke, he smiled weakly and handed Akavak his fur-lined mitts.

Outside, Akavak rolled the staff in the hard snow until it was straight and he could feel it start to freeze. Then he placed it on top of the snowhouse, safe from the teeth of the starving dog.

He stretched himself, glad to be free of the snowhouse after being held so many days a prisoner of the storm. The clouds were breaking open everywhere across the dark sky, and he could see the stars flashing their light down to him. The storm would pass before the true dawn came. This gave Akavak a feeling of hope and almost of joy, though he could not tell why, since they had no dogs, no sled, no food, and they must surely die on top of this lonely mountain.

Shivering with cold and hunger, he crawled back into the little snowhouse and went to sleep, dreaming of soft, delicious marrow from the cracked bones of caribou and the tender flesh of a young loon.

When he awoke, everything was deadly silent, for the wind had gone completely. His grandfather, who was always awake before Akavak, this time lay sound asleep, his face hidden. Only his breath rising in thin steam showed that he was alive. Akavak saw that all the seal oil was gone and the flame in the stone lamp was out. It was bitterly cold in the igloo.

Akavak cut away the door again and crawled out into the light

of morning. A freezing fog had swept in around the mountains, and the peaks above him seemed to hover in the air like giant ghosts. The snow around their house had been carved into weird shapes that flowed into one another. These wind-packed drifts were difficult to see because they cast no shadow in the foggy light.

After replacing the snow door, Akavak walked a little way up the gully. He was stiff and moved slowly. Through the eddying fog, he could see the great plain once again, now blown almost clear of snow. Rocks and gray tundra moss lay exposed from the violence of the wind. He wondered which direction he and his grandfather should follow.

Suddenly he saw them. They loomed out of the fog like footless black monsters with huge humped shoulders. Their heads were down, and their black-tipped horns curved out sharply. At first, he

counted as many as he had fingers on his right hand. Then more appeared, and he saw as many as his fingers on both hands. They were coming straight toward him. He stood as though frozen in his tracks. The biggest animal, the one in the lead, stopped and sniffed the air suspiciously.

Akavak turned. He crouched and moved quickly out of their line of sight. Then he stumbled hurriedly along the gully to the little snowhouse.

"Grandfather! Grandfather!" Akavak called as he crawled into the snowhouse. "There are musk ox. Many of them. Just beyond the gully."

"I cannot stand up this morning, boy," his grandfather said in a quivering voice. "Perhaps it is because I am cramped from not moving, and the lamp is out of oil and it is cold in here. I fell down when I tried to leave the house, and now I cannot rise."

Akavak knelt beside his grandfather and placed his hand on his cheek. It felt cold, and his eyes seemed weak and dim.

"What shall I do, Grandfather? What shall I do?" Akavak said again. "All that meat stands there before us. Can I kill them with the seal harpoon?"

For a long time there was no answer. Then his grandfather said softly, "Never. Their weight would break it like a sliver of thin ice. Bring the rolled skin into the house. Bring me my staff."

Akavak hurried out and returned with the staff.

"Try to bend it," said the old man.

Akavak tried, but it was now frozen solid.

"I cannot bend it," said Akavak. "It is hard as whalebone."

"Good. Now take the sealskin lacings from my boot tops and tie them together. Has the wind blown the tundra moss free of snow?" he asked.

"Yes," said Akavak.

"Good," said his grandfather again. "Then the musk ox have

come up to feed on the high plateau after the storm. They should stay near us for a while."

The old man drew the sharp stone blade from beneath the sleeping skin and tried to bind it to the frozen staff, but he was too weak, and his hands trembled.

"Here, boy, you lash this blade. Do it strongly, mind you, for it could mean your life to have it slip."

When Akavak had bound the rough spearhead into place, his grandfather said, "Now take the water from beneath the ice in the horn cup and pour it over the lashings. Quickly stand the spear outside, and the bindings will swell and freeze."

Having placed the spear outside, Akavak crawled inside the house again, and his grandfather said to him, "Musk ox are strange, lonely beasts who live far from men. Our people do not know well how to hunt them, for we rarely see them. It is wrong that a boy such as you should have to go alone after them while his grandfather rests like a child in the snowhouse. But there is no help for it. Today I could not even crawl to them, and the musk ox are our only chance to live.

"I cannot tell you what these strong animals will do when you go close to them. Sometimes they will attack you, sometimes they will run away from you, and sometimes they will stand on the open plain and form a circle to protect their young. I have never seen them make such a circle, but hunters say it is the worst and most dangerous time of all.

"Do not throw that spear. Keep it, for you may need it a second time. If a musk ox attacks you, kneel and place the butt of the spear firmly on the ground and allow the animal to run onto the point. Here, take my short knife and my hunting bag. Go with strength," he whispered, and he lay down once more in the cold.

Akavak left the snowhouse, quickly replacing the snow door. As he walked up the gully, he said to himself, "I will not return to that igloo until I have food. Only with food will I return."

The fog swirled thickly across the plateau, and Akavak, light-headed with hunger, started to run. He feared that he had lost the herd.

Suddenly the musk ox appeared again through the fog. He was almost beside them, and they snorted in fear and anger at being disturbed by this strange creature. The big bull that led them stood watching beneath the immense curve of its humped shoulders. Its long dark-brown hair trailed almost to the snow, nearly covering short, powerful legs. Its huge horns were joined together by a massive plate of bone that protected the front of its skull from where they swept downward, then curved upward into two sharp points.

Akavak was so close that he could see the bull's nostrils widen as it blew out clouds of breath into the freezing air. Its eyes rolled wildly, showing the whites, as its hoofs angrily flung up clots of snow.

A calf bawled out in alarm. The big bull ran in a short circle, herding the young males, females, and their offspring into a tight group. Shoulder to shoulder they stood, with the calves protected in the middle. Any outside enemy would have to meet their deadly horns.

Akavak knelt down in front of the musk ox. He dug his spear

into the frozen ground and waited. Nothing happened. He called out to them, but still nothing happened. He dared not throw his spear at them, and yet they would not attack him.

Some of the musk ox lost interest because Akavak did not smell or act like their only known enemy, the wolf. They began to eat the rough tundra moss and then broke their circle and started to move down the high plateau. But they were nervous and watchful and kept a good distance between themselves and this stranger.

Akavak trailed after the herd, not knowing how to approach them again. He could see through a clearing in the fog that they would soon cross a part of the glacier, and he feared that he would lose them.

With a desperate shout, he ran straight toward them. The musk ox milled around, and the big bull, with its instinct for protection, once again forced the others into a close circle. They stood heads down, carefully eying Akavak.

Then suddenly they stiffened and shifted their weight, spreading their feet wide, ready for an attack. They snorted nervously, but they did not seem to be watching Akavak any more. Quickly he looked around. He saw a gray form crouched in the snow less than a sled's length from him. Its hair bristled. The end of its tail flipped nervously back and forth. Its yellow eyes seemed to glow with madness.

Akavak stared in wonder and in fright, for it was the dog Kajuq, half crazy with hunger, come to join in the kill. The dog crept forward on its belly like a wolf. Then, with its ears back and a low growl in its throat, it rushed straight at the big bull. It swerved just in time to escape the terrible twisting thrust of the sharp horns. The dog ran in a circle and just as swiftly attacked again. This time the big bull was ready for him. It rushed out of the circle straight at the dog that raced past Akavak. Kajuq was caught between the terrible horns. Before Akavak's eyes, the great beast flung up his head, tossing Kajuq in the air like a child's toy.

The head of the musk ox was still up, exposing its throat, as it rushed at Akavak. Dropping quickly onto one knee, he drove the butt of the spear against the frozen tundra and held fast. He felt the spear shaft buckle in his hands, but not before it had driven the sharply pointed stone blade deep into the animal's throat.

Akavak rolled aside to avoid the sharp flaying hoofs. He watched helplessly as the animal turned to renew its attack, for the

bent spear shaft that lay beside him was without its point. Then he saw the musk ox stagger, and dark artery blood gushed out over the snow. The great bull stumbled to its knees. With a mighty sigh, its spirit rushed out of its body, and it was dead.

The other musk ox had broken their circle, and Akavak saw the last of them disappearing into the swirling mists.

He stood up and walked slowly toward the great black beast that lay on the snow before him. At that moment, he also saw the dog Kajuq limping toward the kill. The two creatures, man and dog, eyed each other. Kajuq reached the fallen animal first and stood there snarling. Akavak raised his hand and called a command to the dog, but it would not obey him.

Weak and starving, Akavak watched the dog slowly eat his fill of the meat. When Kajuq had finished, he stared at Akavak as if in triumph. Then with a low growl, he turned and stalked slowly off into the mist.

Akavak shook with excitement as he knelt, quickly cut away and devoured strips of the warm meat. With his knife, he removed the stone spearhead from the big animal's throat. Then he cut out the liver and removed a heavy layer of rich back fat that he knew would make fuel for the lamp. He severed the spine with the stone blade and cut away the animal's hindquarters. These he tied by the feet to the end of the spear.

Although the load weighed as much as he did, the warm meat had given him strength and hope, and he was eager to get the food back to his grandfather. He found that the meat slipped easily over the hard-packed drifts. The sun was high, showing pale yellow through the mists above him, when he reached the igloo.

"Grandfather! Grandfather! I have meat for you," Akavak called as he cut open the door and crawled inside the snowhouse, dragging the huge hindquarters of the musk ox after him.

The igloo was freezing cold, though it glowed inside with the pale light of the afternoon sun. The old man stared at Akavak from his caribou-skin wrapping. But he was pale, his lips were blue, and he did not speak or seem to recognize him. Akavak gently fed him some soft strips of liver. He then whirled the bow drill until it made smoke and a small flame, and he lighted the old wick and fed it with the back fat from the musk ox. Slowly the fat melted and flowed until the lamp burned brightly, filling the small igloo with warmth and light. Holding the horn cups over the heat, Akavak made a rich blood soup and fed this slowly to his grandfather.

He could see and feel the warmth return to his grandfather's cheeks and hands. Soon the old man smiled, and finally he was able to sit up, and all of his senses returned to him.

Akavak ate more of the delicious meat and trimmed the wick in the lamp so that it would burn throughout the night.

He lay down beside his grandfather. Before he went to sleep, he thought for a long time of his sister, and so vivid were his thoughts that she seemed to appear before him, standing small and alone on the snow, as he had seen her last on the day of his leaving.

In the morning, his grandfather was hungry again. He drank the thick soup they made and ate more meat with Akavak.

When Akavak went out of the snowhouse, he saw the dog lying in the snow. Kajuq stood up, stretched, wriggled his body, and licked his lips in a friendly way.

"Grandfather, the dog is back," called Akavak.

"Good. Feed him some meat," answered his grandfather.

Akavak cut a portion from the lower leg and threw it to Kajuq, who wolfed it down, curled up on the snow, and went to sleep.

Akavak looked up at the sky with a great feeling of relief, for now he believed that they had both escaped from the evil powers of the mountains.

That night in the snowhouse when they ate again, Akavak told his grandfather every detail of the musk-ox hunt and how the dog had helped him.

The old man listened carefully to each word and was silent for a long time. Then, slowly beating time with his hands, he sang an ancient song that he had once heard from the far northern people, the ones who live behind the sun:

"Ayii, Ayii, Ayii,
I wish to see the musk ox run again.
It is not enough for me
To sing of the dear beasts.
Sitting here in the igloo
My songs fade away,
My words melt away,
Like hills in fog.
Ayii, Ayii, Ayii."

"That song is old, and yet its words suit me very well," said the grandfather.

They drifted off to sleep, and Akavak dreamed of the terrible blue abyss. In his dreams, he looked over the edge and imagined he saw the sled floating, suspended forever in blue shadows.

When he awoke, he took Kajuq's long dog line, and the harpoon with its line, and headed toward the glacier. The dog followed him. It took him a little time to find the hole again, for their tracks had been filled in by the storm. When he saw it, he was almost afraid to go near, so vivid and terrible were his memories of that place. He felt his way forward with the harpoon. Then he lay down and crawled to the edge, where he could look into the gaping hole.

There hung the sled, almost as he had seen it in his dream. It was wedged tightly between the icy walls of the giant crack. He thought with sadness of the dogs that must be lying far below under the pile of fallen snow. He studied the position and angle of the sled for some time, noticing that one runner did not touch the ice wall.

Carefully he tied a strong slipknot in the sealskin harpoon line, and this he tied to the end of the long dog line. Holding his breath, he lowered the knotted line and slipped it over the end of the wooden sled runner. Cautiously he drew the line upward until he saw the noose tighten. Then he attached the dog line to Kajuq's harness, and together they pulled the sled free and hauled it slowly out of the crack.

Akavak pushed the sled away from the dangerous hole and danced with delight when he saw that the other dog lines were still attached to it. Also the big white bearskin, the lamp, the extra sleeping skins, and the mitts his sister had given him were still lashed in place.

"With this sled, I shall leave these mountains," he said to himself again and again. "I shall take my grandfather out of these mountains, and we shall go to his brother's land."

When his grandfather looked out of the igloo and saw the sled, he sat up and said in a trembling voice, "I had given up hope of seeing my brother, but look, the mountain spirits may wish to give us back our lives again." And he clapped his hands with joy.

That night his grandfather crawled out of the snowhouse and stood up, supporting himself with the harpoon shaft as he leaned against Akavak. The sky was clear and full of stars. The old man looked up and pointed at the bright north star, then lowered his arm straight down until his shaking finger pointed to a narrow pass between two hills.

"There, through that pass we shall travel north again across the plateau. Below that star lies the giant river Kuujjuaq that flows past my brother's camp."

Akavak fed the dog well and crawled into the snowhouse. In preparation for the journey, he began cutting wide strips from the bearskin with which to fashion a harness for himself. He sharpened a needle from a splinter of musk-ox bone and drew fine strong sinew from the musk-ox leg. With these he sewed the harness together. His sewing was crude, for all sewing in their camp was done by the women, and he wished that his mother could be there to help him.

In the morning, he harnessed the dog, loaded the lamp and the precious meat, and with the bearskin made a comfortable place for his grandfather to lie on the sled. When this was done, he helped the old man out of the snowhouse and urged him to lie down on the sled, while he carefully covered him with skins.

All that day Akavak and the dog struggled across the high plateau, and so hard did they work that they did not feel the biting cold. When the sun set and the mountains cast blue shadows across the snow, they stopped to build a snowhouse. But the old man was so paralyzed by the cold that he could not help. Akavak

worked alone until the igloo was completed. It took him a long time to light the lamp and to feed his grandfather, for now he had to do everything by himself.

"Tomorrow, if the wind does not rise, we will reach the far edge of the mountain. Tomorrow. Tomorrow," the old man mumbled again and again.

On the following day, it was much warmer, without a breath of wind, and Akavak's grandfather seemed stronger. He sat up on the sled and even tried to push with his hands to ease the load when they crossed a difficult drift.

All day Akavak pulled beside the sled dog, Kajuq. Akavak's harness cut into his shoulders painfully, and he thought at times that

he could walk no more. But in his mind he kept thinking, "We are closer now. This journey nears its end."

Slowly they made their way forward through the twilight until they rounded a small hill. There lay the sight they had so long awaited. It was the end of the plateau. Akavak's grandfather let out a broken cry of triumph. The mountains were behind them, and the snow-covered plateau ended sharply against a line of sky.

"That is the edge. I remember the edge," he cried.

Even the tired dog seemed to understand and strained against the harness until darkness, when they reached the very edge of the plateau where the mountain slopes ran down toward the sea.

The small igloo Akavak built that night was quick and crude, for he planned to leave it as soon as there was light. They fed the dog and ate the musk-ox flesh again and slept. Akavak awoke once in the night, hearing his grandfather call out his brother's name as he moaned and turned in the darkness.

Dawn came slowly into the eastern sky, lighting the cracks in the dome of the snowhouse. Akavak cut away the door and crawled out. In all his life, he had never seen such a sight. The immense sky stretched around him like an endless blue bowl spanning the land and the frozen sea. As he watched, the coast far below turned pink and gold in the first rays of the morning sun.

"Look! Look! The river. The Kuujjuaq," cried the old man who had crawled out beside his grandson.

"And there are the snowhouses," said Akavak, pointing to a place near the sea. "Up here the land is still held in the grip of winter, but down below on the coast, there are signs of spring."

"Now," said his grandfather. "Now comes the hardest part of all, for the snow on the mountainside is deep and treacherous, with countless rocks hidden from our view. If the sled goes too fast and you lose control, all will be lost.

"Cut half of the bearskin into wide strips and twist them together into a great rope to hold loose in front of the runners. That will help to slow us down. Break the harpoon shaft and lash both halves together across the front of the sled so you can have a pair of handles to hold on to and guide us. Tie the dog on a short line, and be sure his harness is tight. He will be afraid and will help us to hold back the sled.

"I am ashamed that I cannot help you. You must lash me tightly to the sled, for if I fall off, you will not be able to stop and return for me."

Akavak made the preparations. He noticed when he started to draw the long lashings tight that his grandfather turned away his face and quickly drew his right hand free, for he hated to be completely bound and helpless in the face of such danger.

A moment later he turned to Akavak once more and said softly, "I believe now that I may reach my brother's camp. For me it is like returning home again, as I shall see my younger brother in the land of our youth. Just now, like a dream before my eyes, I seemed to see again the two of us running across the soft tundra during the midsummer moon. We were chasing the big molting ganders with their black necks outstretched. I fell first into a shallow pond, and my brother laughed so hard that he fell in beside me. That is how life was with us when we were growing up. We were never apart.

"But best of all," said his grandfather, "I believe now that you will live to walk beyond these mountains, that you will return to our family, and that your children will carry within them the spirits of their ancestors."

"*Iingujuksaujuq*. It should be so," answered Akavak.

Holding the harpoon handles, Akavak cautiously eased the heavily loaded sled over the edge of the steep downward slope. He lay out almost flat on his back, digging his heels into the snow before him. The dog howled in terror and drew back behind the sled, digging his paws into the snow, fighting to break their downward speed.

Akavak flung the twisted bearskin rope under the runners.

When the strain was so great that Akavak thought he must let go or have his arms dragged from their sockets, they struck a big stone, swerved, and halted. He had to fling his weight against the sled to prevent it from rolling over. Here they rested among the sharp black rocks, exposed by the recent windstorm. He looked at his grandfather, lashed to the sled, almost hidden in the fur robes, and the old man smiled weakly and nodded to him.

Fearfully Akavak started the sled on the last terrible run down the mountain. He cut across the slope, and then, with a tremendous effort, he turned the sled and went in the other direction, leaving a large zigzag trail on the mountainside. Again he used the twisted bearskin beneath the runners to break their speed.

Then suddenly the slowing rope slipped from his grasp. Akavak lost control, and the heavy sled rushed down the mountain, dragging Akavak and Kajuq with it. It thundered over glare ice, flew silently over deep snow, and did not stop until it hit some bare rocks. There it almost overturned, but its speed was halted, and Akavak gained control once more.

He was wet with sweat. Snow was packed in his sleeves and filled the neck of his parka. But as he wiped his face clean and looked back at his long curving track down the mountain, he saw that the worst was past. Before him lay the flat coast and the giant river that flowed into the sea. They were saved.

Akavak drove his weight against the sled once more and knelt on the side, pushing with one foot. The sled moved so fast that it passed the dog, who raced forward trying to keep out of the way of the bounding runners.

Akavak could see the people of the tiny village hurrying out of their houses and running toward him in great excitement, for they had never seen a loaded sled pulled by one dog arrive from the mountains.

Their momentum carried the sled right into the middle of the camp, where the people clustered. The strange dogs circled and sniffed and snarled at Kajuq, but he stood aloof among them like a lean gray wolf.

An old man came forward, his arms upraised in greeting. He called out, "Relative! Nephew of mine. You have arrived."

Akavak got off the sled and said to him, "We have arrived, great-uncle of mine. At last I see you."

They stood before each other, and Akavak saw that this man was almost the image of his grandfather.

Whirling, he started to undo the lines he had so carefully tied to hold his grandfather on the sled. The others gathered around him. Quickly Akavak turned back the caribou skin that half covered the old man's face. His grandfather's eyes were still open, but now they stared blankly at the sky, seeing nothing. Akavak felt his cheek. It was freezing cold. He grasped his grandfather's hand, but that, too, was icy cold. The white clutched fingers seemed to reach out as if in readiness to greet his brother.

Akavak's whole body began to tremble and shake as though he stood naked in a freezing wind. His throat was so tight that he could not speak. Silently he pointed at the stiffened hand.

His great-uncle bent down and gently covered his brother's face with the caribou skin. The women in the camp huddled together, and from them rose a great wailing as they drew their hoods over their faces. Then there was silence.

The brother pulled away the last lashing that held Akavak's grandfather to the sled. He raised his arms slowly and sang out in a strong voice:

"Ayii, Ayii,
Arise, arise,
With movements
Swift as a raven's wing,
Arise to meet the day.
Turn your face
From the dark of night
To gaze at the dawn
As it whitens the sky.
Arise, arise,
Ayii, Ayii."

Akavak looked once more at the form of his grandfather, lying lifeless on the sled, then turned away with a terrible feeling of loneliness.

The old women and some young girls led him up to the big sealskin tent that stood on a dry gravel bank, near the winter snow-houses that now were crumbling in the warmth of the spring sun. A small flock of snowbirds migrating from the south landed near the tent. Torrents of water from the melting snow cut curving paths toward the sea. Everywhere around him were the soft signs of spring, as the new season advanced across the land. To Akavak it seemed as though the whole world was being born again.

Before he entered the tent, he turned and looked up at the mountains. They stood like ancient giants guarding some forbidden place. White clouds soared across their peaks. The mountains were different for him now. He had climbed them and lived within them. He had almost died there. From those great heights, he had looked down at the world like a wind spirit and had seen all of the land and the vast distances of the frozen sea. After that he had come down from the mountains. But now, like his grandfather, he had a strong secret feeling for the white plateau. And he knew that his vision of the great black beasts running on the high plain would stay with him forever.

He entered and sat down wearily on the soft skins that covered the wide bed, and the young women removed his damp boots and stood shyly near him. In the warmth of the tent, he drank the hot brown soup they offered him and ate the delicate meat of a young seal.

He stared into the flame of the big stone lamp, watching it shimmer and dance like waves on the sea in summer. No longer did he tremble from cold and fear and hunger. He lay back on the warm caribou skins, and as he fell asleep, he dreamed that he took his grandfather's hand and together they soared upward—upward and across the ancient mountains, over the whiteness of the glacier, and out among the stars.

WOLF RUN

To save his strength, Panniq had slept through the long morning and most of the freezing afternoon. Now, with the coming of twilight, he heard the first pounding of the big drum. With it, from another igloo, came his uncle's toneless singing, followed by an answering chorus, a wailing of women's voices. Their song of hunger seemed to gain strength as it drifted upward into the clear night sky.

Only three snowhouses stood in this camp where Panniq lived, three lonely igloos just beginning to crumble in the first faint warmth of spring.

Almost all of Panniq's people were his relatives, caribou hunters, nomads on the treeless plain. They were clever bowmen and spearmen, dancers and singers, and dog-team drivers.

Far away beyond them lived other humans. To the south on the edge of the forest lived the Allaitt, tall, frightening First Nations people, swift snowshoe men, who pulled long, thin toboggans over the soft snow that piled waist deep among the whispering trees.

To the east along the barren shores of the salt sea lived the Aivilingmiut, the walrus people, fearless hunters of those great ivory-tusked beasts.

Far to the west lived the Umingmangmiut, the musk-ox people, hard-running bowmen who stalked the heavy horned animals on the high plain.

To the north lived the Nattilingmiut, the seal hunters, listeners at the breathing places in the ice. Their stone lamps burned bright with rich seal oil, and their finely sewn sealskin boots held out water.

Panniq's grandfather had heard that strange pale people lived south of the First Nations people. They were iron knife makers, bead makers, and great travelers, some said, but he had never seen them.

During the years of Panniq's growing, there had always been great haunches of caribou lying frozen white in the meat porches of their igloos or piled high beside their tents in summer. But in the past Panniq's people had known starvation at the end of the winter moons. Famine had caused the death of many of his relatives. Now such a dangerous time had come again, threatening to destroy their whole camp. The spring migration of caribou had failed them. The caribou herd had not returned from the south. All those years of plenty had disappeared, perhaps forever, in the thirteenth spring of Panniq's life. Misfortune and famine had come to haunt his people like the black shadow from a raven's wing.

Bad fortune had struck them first when Panniq's father had died in the summer past. It had happened at the swift river crossing during the caribou hunting. At that time everyone in the whole camp had walked through the long days and clear white nights, cautiously bringing together the wide-ranging caribou that were grazing across the tundra plain. As was their custom, they slowly herded the caribou into a path that led to the river between the *inuksuit*, stone images built long ago by their forefathers to look like men. This they did so cleverly that the animals were not aware of what was happening until it was too late. When the caribou finally arrived at the narrows in the river, they had no other place to go and

no choice but to swim. This slowed them up, and it was here that Panniq's father, with his killing spear in hand, met them in his slim kayak. A big bull caribou, leading the others across the swollen current, panicked when he saw the hunter. He lunged at the kayak, cutting it with his sharp hoofs and overturning it. In the rush of freezing water, Panniq's father was drowned. Perhaps because of this, the whole autumn hunt had gone badly.

His father's death was the worst thing that could have happened to Panniq's family. Now there was only his grandfather and himself trying to feed the women of their household: his grandmother, his mother with a new baby still carried in a warm pouch on her back, and his young sister, Sila. Of course, his uncles who lived in the other two igloos helped the family when they could, but they, too,

had many mouths to feed and would have no food now until the caribou returned.

Panniq's name meant prime bull caribou, one whose sides bulge with strength and good health, one whose coat is glossy. It was a name that had come down to him from a great-uncle. In good times it suited him perfectly.

He was tall and strong for his age because he had been given rich red caribou meat to eat throughout his whole life. He had long blue-black hair that hung on either side of his smooth, wide-jawed face. When Panniq laughed, his dark eyes shone and his strong teeth flashed white against his tanned skin. He had almost reached his full strength and could run a sled and dogs as well as most men. He could drive an arrow to its mark with increasing sureness.

But how could these skills help his family now, with no dogs left alive in the camp and no game for his bow? His strength had

gone from him, and the dreaded fear of hunger filled his mind. What could he do?

Panniq's grandfather had been a clever hunter in his day, but that time had long passed. Now the old man lay helpless and alone, wrapped in furs, slowly starving on the wide bed, too weak even to walk to the nearest igloo to help his relatives with their magic chanting that begged the caribou to return to the empty land.

It was dark and freezing cold inside the igloo. There was not even one small scrap of caribou fat to burn as fuel in the stone lamp. Panniq stared through the gloom at his grandfather and knew that the old man was awake and listening to the steady pleading beat of the drum. How Panniq longed to give him food and heat and light again!

Panniq rose painfully from his place in the family bed. He was fully dressed, but his clothing was old. The tears in it had been sewn and resewn by his mother, who had no caribou hides to make new garments for the family. Next to his skin Panniq wore pants and a parka and long stockings made from caribou fawn skins, all with the soft hair turned in toward his body. Over these, because it was winter, Panniq wore heavier caribou-skin clothing, parka, pants, and boots, with the hair turned out against the cold. A double hood protected his head and allowed him to turn his face away from the freezing wind. He also had double fur mitts.

When Panniq put on all of his clothes, it was as though he had built a soft warm house around himself, so perfectly were they designed to protect him from the stinging cold. If he ran and grew too warm, he needed only to push back his hood a little or remove one mitt, and this would gently cool his whole body.

Sadly Panniq turned and made his way up through the winding snow-block entrance passage. Outside the igloo, when he first breathed in the sharp freshness of the night air, his head felt light. He was dizzy and sick with hunger. The cold seemed to reach inside his worn-out parka and run its icy hands along his spine. He shuddered as he pulled up his hood and listened to the steady pounding of the big flat drum and thought of his mother and grandmother and his sister, Sila, weakly wailing in their hunger, calling to the lost caribou in their singsong voices, calling to them somewhere out on the distant barrens. Panniq knew that he, too, was dying, that his bones would turn white and disappear like dust with all the rest if the caribou did not come to them before the moon was full again.

In his mind's eye, Panniq could see the caribou far away in the darkness, moving northward in great herds like silent ghosts against the whiteness of the snow. Above their backs the moonlight caught the cloud of vapor formed by their breathing and spun it into a silver sheen.

He flung his hands out toward the dance house and said aloud, "I will not wait here and watch us die like helpless children. I will go walking, searching for the caribou. I shall go out and find our relatives, the ones living three days' dog-team journey west of us, those who dwell between the two lakes. They have a clever way of catching many fish and storing them beneath a pile of stones. Even

if the caribou have not come to them, they should have many big lake trout left from their spearing in the autumn moon.

"I will go now while I still have a little strength, for I can almost see those fat hook-jawed trout, half as long as I am, lying frosted white beneath the stones of the cache. I can almost taste the sweet flesh thawing in my throat. These relatives of ours will surely send me back with dogs and a sled and enough fish to feed the people in this camp."

Panniq turned swiftly back into the igloo and gathered together his father's hunting equipment. His father's knife, bow and arrows, and killing spear were all made of caribou bones, bent or straightened, bound with caribou sinew, and fitted carefully with pounded copper points. Everything that Panniq's people needed came from the caribou or could easily be found in the country around them.

"Grandfather of mine," Panniq called out, "I am going away. I am going walking into the west to find caribou or fish for us. Unless I do this, I believe that everything will soon be ended here."

"That may be so, grandson of mine, but what you wish to do is not our custom. Have patience, wait for the magic of the drum to bring the caribou to us."

"I have tried, but I cannot believe in magic, Grandfather. I believe that only these arrows and this spear, or perhaps our neighbors' gift of food, can save us from starving."

"Life is not so simple as that," said his grandfather, "but I am old and sick and may not rise again. You must choose your own way to live or die. You must now decide how best to help this family.

"Remember the things that we have taught you," his grandfather added. "Remember that my thoughts will travel with you out

across the wide plain. That is all I can do for this family. My body lies helpless on this bed. Only my thoughts have the strength to fly with you."

Panniq turned away sadly, certain that he would not see his grandfather again. When he left the snowhouse, he gathered all his strength for this impossible journey. He slashed a narrow piece of skin from his caribou boot top, stuffed it in his mouth, and chewed it to ease his hunger.

With determination he started walking westward, not daring to say farewell to his mother or grandmother or his sister, Sila, fearing that this might rob him of his courage. Panniq knew that just one blizzard, one violent windstorm, would kill him. He would freeze to death out there on the plain, for he carried no fire, no fuel to heat himself against the cold, and he was using up his last strength. He walked a long way before he could no longer hear the distant throbbing sound of the drum.

When he came to the wolf run, he stopped and examined it carefully, remembering that it was almost a sacred place to his

grandparents. The wolf run stretched west along a low snow ridge, ending at a big den where a female had borne her pups many springs before. This den was no longer used for raising families, but for some curious reason the wolves had chosen it as a meeting place. Their big splayfooted tracks lay one upon the other in a worn and narrow trail along the whole length of the ridge. They came to the wolf run, of course, to find a mate. But also, perhaps they came because, like humans, they sometimes wished to be in company with others, to play, to argue, and to sing together when the moon was full.

When Panniq had walked the length of the wolf run and come near the den, he noticed a trail of human footprints that, like his own, curved in from the direction of the camp and, beside them, a trail of footprints returning. These tracks seemed to fall in step with

the big four-toed wolf prints, and Panniq knelt down to examine them. The imprints were light, for the walker was not heavy. The insteps were high and the steps were short. Each footprint toed in, in the way of a woman walking. Yes, these were certainly the footprints of his grandmother. It could be no one else.

Panniq rose and hurried away into the west, but as he walked, he was troubled. He wished that he could turn back and ask his

grandmother about her visit to the wolf run. He knew that she had been giving her food to Sila for nearly half a moon so that she had lost strength quickly herself. Yet in the moonlight he had seen that the footprints were so sharp and fresh and clear that they must have been made that very night.

The moon had risen and cast a pale glow across the snow, forming a long shining path of light that spread before him. Panniq stood beneath the stars and listened quietly. Far to the west he heard the lonely howl of a wolf, and this was faintly answered by another. Perhaps it was a hunting signal or just a cry of hunger, as the wolves, like Panniq, searched for the caribou that might not come in time.

As he walked on throughout the freezing night, Panniq felt the bulge of each of his amulets. Inside his parka his grandmother had carefully sewn three of them; they were tightly hidden beneath patches of skin, and he had never seen them, but his mother had whispered that one was a wolf's claw and another a hawk's bill, to make him a swift hunter like his father and his grandfather, and that these were both wrapped in musk-ox hair to keep him warm. She would never say what amulet was hidden beneath the third patch.

Panniq walked light-footed, sometimes laughing, sometimes singing or talking foolishly to himself, trying to forget his terrible pangs of hunger, trying to forget that life was running out of him. He imagined that his strength dripped away into the snow, like warm water oozing from his feet, filling every footstep he left behind.

He watched the white dawn come slowly, lighting up the east-

ern sky, and in the true morning the sun rose and flooded the world
with a bright, cold light. Panniq stopped and squatted on his heels.
He rested, watching a raven chase its mate across the lonely sky.
The two thin black birds dived and turned, rolling over each other
in silent, swift-winged delight. Ravens were always hungry, it was
said, but they could grow thin and yet remain alive after every other
living thing had perished.

When the sun stood high in the eastern sky and Panniq felt its
warmth upon his back, he looked for a small open patch of tundra
that the spring winds had blown clear of snow, where he might
kneel and sleep. With his knife he cut two large flat blocks of snow
and set them up for protection against the sharpness of the rising

breeze. He knelt down, and, placing one mitt under each knee, he drew his arms inside his parka and buried his face deep in his fur hood. He went to sleep kneeling with his head on his arms, for he did not dare to rest his whole body against the freezing ground.

The day was almost gone when he awoke, half mad with hunger. His stomach burned like fire, and he had to pull his hair as hard as he could to make himself feel a different kind of pain and to drive himself up onto his feet to go forward.

As he stumbled onward, he stared at the blood-red ball of sun that slid slowly down into the freezing grayness of the western sky. The whole fat land seemed empty and white, without shadows. It was silent, save for his walking and the snow squealing beneath

his feet, laughing at him, telling him that his search was hopeless. So great was his desire to eat that he gnawed a hole in the wrist of his left sleeve, scarcely bothering to spit out the worn caribou hairs.

He continued to march westward throughout the long star-filled night. Again he heard the lonely howl of a wolf and far away an answering call. He knew these were not the sharp signals of wolves hunting and running on the scent of meat, just howls of hunger into the darkness. Perhaps, like the drummers and the women's chorus in Panniq's camp, these wolves were trying to call the caribou back into the land.

At dawn Panniq saw something that sent him running forward in wild excitement. He fell onto his knees when he reached the scattered black droppings of an Arctic hare that had rested there five nights before. He gobbled up every one of them that he could find, and to make a meal of it, he cut away the top of his other boot and chewed the skin. He ate snow to ease his thirst and give his body water, and for a little while his hunger went away, enough to let him sleep again briefly through the weak warmth of another day.

He dreamed that he was walking once again at his grand-mother's side. She was old and strong and wise, and in all his life Panniq would never forget the days at the end of winter when she had always taken him with his sister to wander across the rolling stretches of the tundra plain in search of every sign of life. She knew the very day when the big flocks of white-cheeked geese would return to the land. She knew when the bright new flowers

would burst forth, turning the whole plain into an endless sea of color.

As they walked together, small flocks of snowbirds would rise before them and fly away like the whirling snowflakes of winter. From near and far they would hear, *"Kum-iaq, kum-iaq,"* the throbbing call of the white-feathered male ptarmigan, and the soft answering calls of the females, *"Gitavau, gitavau."*

During their wanderings, their grandmother told them many things, and Panniq and his sister came to understand the land in a new way. She taught them how to find their way, how to mark their path and to know the changing moods of lake and sky. She taught them how to smell the air, to test the shifting breeze, to watch the clouds for warnings of a coming storm. She taught them silence and patience, how to stalk the animals with care, how to know what they were thinking. "How fast will that hare run," she would ask, "and when, and in which direction?"

She urged them to study each bird and know how long it would sit and when it would fly. She told them how the loon had gained its spots, and she cried out, imitating the wild laughing of the loon. She spoke to them about the piercing yellow eyes of the golden eagles that swing in wide-winged circles high above the plain. She spoke of the small, brave short-tailed lemming that will stand and fight a barren ground grizzly bear to protect its young, and of the wild courage of the long-necked swans that come each spring to nest on the tundra.

She told them that caribou had at first been only tufts of grass, but when the white raven brought light into the world, they had been set free in their countless numbers to rove the earth from the dwarfed forests in the south to the frozen ocean that stretched across the north, bringing food to men.

All of these things she taught Panniq and his sister, who were a part of her continuing family. She carried ancient knowledge deep inside herself, wisdom that women have always possessed, wisdom that they have carefully handed down to their children and grandchildren since the beginning of mankind.

Panniq's grandmother's face was old and brown and finely seamed like leather, and her hands were blunt and strong, with delicate blue tattoo lines on her wrists. She had seen long hard winters when, with a child on her back, she, like the others, had been forced to help the dogs drag the sleds through deep snow to new hunting places. She had watched endless new spring suns come and flood the land, turning the whole world into a blinding white bowl of brightness. Still her dark eyes were clear and quick as those of a young fox. When Panniq's grandmother smiled, her white teeth flashed square and strong, worn short from chewing countless caribou skins into soft material to be ready for the clever stitches of her precious copper needle.

Panniq dreamed of the times when the men were off hunting and the women and other children were away egg gathering. Then Sila would ask their grandmother to unwrap her treasures hidden in a bundle of caribou skin.

First the old woman would slap the thongs that bound her most precious possessions and call out some magic words. Then she would take out her beautiful headband and carefully polish the shining plate of hammered copper. She would bind this across her forehead, allowing the fox teeth to hang down beside her wide cheekbones. To make her braids hang stiff and thick as deer legs, she would cleverly weave her long black hair around two smooth sticks, and around these braids she would tightly bind long, elegant strings of precious trade beads, bright red and blue and white. Finally when her hair was done, she would carefully pull on her splendid white caribou-skin parka from which all the hair had been removed. Its long, delicate fringes swayed and trembled.

That was the best time of all. When she was elegantly dressed, she began to sing and tell stories. She spoke of the great dance houses, igloos of tremendous size, where she had danced in this costume before their mother had been born. Sila shivered with excitement, and Panniq sat as proud and observant as a dozen hunters in front of his grandmother, who swayed back and forth, holding Sila to her breast. As if by magic, Panniq saw her as a young woman again, smooth-cheeked and beautiful, singing until the sun and moon and stars stopped to listen to the wonder of her words.

At last she spoke of the proudly beautiful blue wolves that run free together, hunting in pairs on the open plain. She told them

how she and their grandfather had often walked together on the wolf run when the first spring moon rode through the sky, for it was like a sacred place to them, a place where life begins. But that was long ago, she said, when they were both young, even before Panniq's mother or father had been born.

When Sila asked her, their grandmother would look around to see that no one else was listening, and then she would tip back her head and howl softly, so like a wolf that it sent shivers up and down their spines. In his dream of hunger, that is how Panniq remembered her.

On the fourth night of walking, Panniq noticed a long thin line of tracks crossing the snow, stretching far out before him. As he approached, he could see that it was the trail of a white fox. Each footprint was carefully placed one in front of the other to form a long, curving arrow pointing westward. Panniq thought the track had been made perhaps three nights before, for he could see where the lightly blown snow had started to fill in each delicate imprint. He gladly followed the track since it went his way and made him feel less lonely.

He had walked for some time beside the track when he saw where the fox had caught the scent of something, for the trail of footprints veered sharply to the right. Panniq turned and followed them. He could already see the place where the fox had been digging in the snow. He knelt beside the hole and looked at the empty, broken eggshells. Panniq envied the fox its keen nose and senses that could smell those frozen eggs lying in last summer's nest beneath the snow. He examined the shells with care. The fox had found and eaten two goose eggs.

Panniq started to dig wildly with his mitted hands, for he knew that a goose lays more than two eggs. At first his digging yielded nothing, but just when he was about to give up, his hand struck something round and smooth. Snatching off his mitt, he removed the big greenish-colored goose egg from the snow. Then setting it

aside, he dug carefully until he had uncovered all the bare ground around the nest. There were no more eggs.

He sat back on his heels and stared with pleasure at his one frozen egg. It was probably rotten inside, but that did not matter at all. He was so hungry that the egg seemed to him a smooth, shining treasure, the most beautiful sight that he had ever seen. With care he picked away half of the shell, exposing one end of the icy yellowish contents.

Slowly he started to suck the egg, feeling the strong flavor trickle into his mouth. It was delicious. He squatted in this way, warming the egg between his mitted hands, then sucking it and looking along the little fox track leading into the west. Then he whispered, "*Matna, matna.* Thank you, thank you for showing me the place where you found food for me." It did not matter that the little fox had gone three long nights ago. Panniq believed that because there was no one, nothing, in the space between them, somehow the little fox might hear and understand him.

He walked on along the line of tracks, sucking the egg that gave him strength to reach a dry patch of tundra. There he slept until the sun sank into the freezing gloom and the chill of night drove him to his feet again and sent him marching once more into the west. As he walked, great moving curtains of light appeared, filling the sky as though they were blown by giant spirits who rushed unseen among the stars.

Panniq's long march through the fifth night was the worst of all, for a sharp, biting wind blew out of the west, leaving white frost patches on his face and chilling him to the bone. It was hard for him to force himself to walk against the wind, and yet he knew he must go on, for if he lay down, the cold would kill him. He could feel the energy he had from the egg going out of him.

He thought about his family lying hungry in their igloo, and he said aloud, "At least they are saving their strength. At least they are not walking themselves to death on this endless plain. If they are careful, they will live for a long time after I am gone."

Toward the end of day, he saw a long ridge that seemed to stretch across the whole country, and when he reached its crest, he rubbed his eyes to make sure that what he saw in the distance was really there. In the twilight before him stretched a great snow-covered lake, and up at the northern end was a frozen river leading to another huge lake, now almost hidden in the cold blue shadows of the evening. There at the narrows he saw two long upright pieces of driftwood that men had planted in the snow to mark their camp.

His stomach seemed to turn over and suck in against his spine as he started to run down the long slope toward the camp. He saw some dark objects lying near two snowhouses. Were they dogs, he wondered? But why was there no warm vapor of life rising from the short snow chimneys in the two igloos? Then, as he caught sight of a huge stone food cache, he forgot everything. The cache was even bigger than he had imagined and must hold fish beyond his counting. His mouth filled with hot juices as he thought of the way his teeth would rip the first bite out of a big trout's belly. In his mind he thought how he would stand them up, frozen, in the snow.

It seemed to Panniq that it took forever, but finally he found himself stumbling up the stone sides of the big cache. Gasping in

horror, he cried out, for the entire top of the cache had been ripped open. He stared into its vast, yawning emptiness. Not a fish head, not a tail, not a fin had been left for him. Inside there were only footprints and frozen urine stains of the dogs that had lived in there for days, fighting each other for the privilege of hungrily licking up every last fishbone.

Panniq whirled around and ran desperately toward the two snowhouses, hoping that the black marks that looked like dogs would rush at him, howling in anger. But nothing moved, and he discovered that the imagined dogs were only a broken stone lamp and several useless pieces of driftwood.

Panniq stopped. He looked cautiously at the two snowhouses. There was a strange quietness about them that he did not like. Everything seemed normal except that the houses were without dogs, without people, and their entrance passages were partly drifted in with snow. No steaming breath of life rose from either of the small snow chimneys above the square ice windows.

Panniq started cautiously to circle the nearest igloo. Then he stopped in horror. There, leaning in a snowdrift, with his right arm outstretched and pointing to the west, was a man who had once visited Panniq's camp. He was called Kanaalaq. Now his face was frozen hard as stone, and the inside of his hood was packed with snow. Against his back a long, hard drift had formed. Panniq knew he could not be alive. Yet why did he alone remain standing there like a sleepwalker, his frozen fingers pointing blindly into the west?

"*Ilakka. Ilakka.* Relatives. Relatives," called Panniq.

But no answer came to him. Only his own voice echoed back to him from the dark half-buried tunnels of the two snowhouses.

"Ilakka. Ilakka," he called out a second time.

But again there was no answer except for the lonely moaning of the wind. No man or woman or child or dog remained alive in this place.

Panniq whirled away from the camp and stumbled wildly into the west, his heart pounding with fear. He looked back only once and saw the dead man pointing at him. Around him stretched a vast frozen loneliness, and for the third time Panniq heard a wolf howl.

That night the wind died, and the pale moon raced through the high clouds. Panniq hobbled onward like an old man, using the killing spear to support himself. With each step he counted a fin-

ger on his hand: *atausiq,* one, *marruuk,* two, *pingasut,* three, *sita-mat,* four, *tallimat,* five. He counted the fingers of his other hand, and when he had counted all his fingers, he would stop and rest briefly, and listen. Then he would force himself on, fearing the frozen man pointing at his back, fearing the wolf that must be following him.

Now he knew how much he feared to die all by himself on this lonely, freezing plain. But on that night and the one that followed, he heard nothing save the ghostlike whispering of the wind as it crept like a pale wolf along the hard, sharp edges of the snowdrifts. It cracked his lips and made each breath sear his nostrils. If he dared to cry, his eyelashes would freeze together so he could not see.

When the sun rose above the white plain, some warmth came into the land once more, and the hard snow grew softer. A silver fog spread over the far horizon and slowly covered the whole land. Once he saw a huge snowy owl sitting on a stone, boldly staring at him through the mist. Panniq tried to notch an arrow to his bow, but his numb fingers would not work for him, and he stood, helpless, as the owl spread its soft wide wings and flew away searching for food.

The fog made Panniq feel that he was walking in a strange dream, and his mind seemed to run away from him and dance backward along his staggering trail of footprints, swooping like the owl, until it reached the camp. There he once again saw his sister, Sila, who was carrying their mother's new baby on her back, pretending she was grown up, and helping their grandmother to peg caribou skins for drying on the summer tundra. In his waking dream Panniq saw his mother step from a new caribou-skin summer tent and call to him. And he answered her, "Yes, yes, here I am. I am coming to you." He could smell rich caribou meat simmering in its thick yellow broth, cooking on the little heather fire she had made. He started running and shouting, "Yes, yes, mother of mine. I am coming back to you. Give me the musk-ox horn cup that I may drink the broth. Give me meat. Give me meat. Give me marrow from the dear caribou bones."

Panniq was really running. Only when he stumbled and fell did he wake up and fight back the tears that came into his eyes, for, of course, his mother was not there and his grandmother and his sister were not there and the food and the fire were gone. He was alone, without even a dream to help him. He was six nights' walking away from their camp. He knew that he was dying and that they, too, must still be starving in the camp. He wished now that he had heeded his grandfather's words and stayed with his people and been content to sing and drum for the caribou with the others, even if they never came. Nothing, he thought, nothing could be worse than the loneliness of dying all by himself out on the frozen whiteness of this inhuman plain.

Panniq came to his senses again, and he heard himself singing aloud and drumming his hands on his thighs. He said to himself, "Be careful, you may be going mad. Disgusting things taste good to you. The freezing wind feels warm to you. You shout aloud and frighten the caribou. Your mind may wander away and never return to you."

When Panniq raised his head, he saw along the snow, not far before him, some footprints, fresh human footprints. He could scarcely believe it. He stood up swaying with weakness. This was no dream, no madness. The path stretched clearly along the whole length of the ridge and disappeared before him. He thought he must be near another camp.

He ran forward, loosely, like a skeleton in tattered rags, for his boots hung loose and his sleeves were ragged where he had eaten the wrists away. When he reached the human track, he fell down

on top of it trying to feel the warmth of some other human rising from the imprints. He crawled along the track to the top of the ridge. There he stopped and stared with horror, for he could see that the footprints led around in a great circle.

He placed his own foot into one of the prints, and when he found that it fitted perfectly, he screamed like a wounded animal, and he shook his fists at the leaden sky and the countless rolling ridges on the treeless plain. He thought that he was lost forever, wasting his strength, walking in useless circles like a madman. He fell down on the snow and lay there sobbing in his weakness.

But soon he felt his jaw muscles twitching. A little fire seemed to burn in his chest, and he said aloud, "Not yet. Not yet. I am not dead yet."

He turned his back to the rising sun and trudged once more into the west, staggering as he went. He set his mind to search for more round black hare droppings, but all he found was snow to ease his thirst.

He marched onward all day through the gray shapelessness of the Arctic fog. All hope of finding caribou had left him. Slowly he made his way up a long rise that crested in a wind-swept gravel ridge that stretched north and south beyond his view. On the ridge he fell down again, his arms covering his face. He looked up once, but seeing nothing, almost hoping that it would be for the last time, he fell asleep. In the long twilight a sharp wind came and blew against him from the west, and clouds drifted in and blotted out the moon.

Panniq's head jerked up, perhaps from some bad dream. As he tried to focus his eyes on the land before him, he saw many spots, dark moving objects. He closed his eyes and pulled his hair, then opened them again. What he saw was not a dream. He could see long lines of dark silver spots moving along the horizon from the south. Chains of caribou were crossing the ridges, coming too late into the land when he was too weak to save his family or even himself.

Panniq cautiously raised up onto his knees and, swaying in the cold wind, stared into the gathering gloom. For a long time he watched the caribou out on the plain. The sky was blown almost clear of clouds, and the moon rode free once more among the stars.

A quick, half-seen movement made Panniq look around in fear, and there within one leap lay a wolf. At first it looked like a stone, windswept of snow. It was huge in size, as long as Panniq himself, almost too big for a wolf, he thought, but as it lay flat, crouched along the snow, tense, ready to spring upon him, Panniq saw its great round eyes blink like yellow orbs reflecting the moonlight. It was very real.

As Panniq watched, in helpless terror, he saw its long lips curl back into a snarl, revealing the deadly knife-shaped teeth. The long dark mantle of guard hairs on the wolf's shoulders trembled in the breeze. The black tip of its tail twitched dangerously back and forth across the snow.

His bow and killing spear lay near him, but Panniq did not have the will or strength to pick them up. Neither did Panniq have the desire to resist the wolf. He knew he could not run away from it, and for fear of falling, he did not even try to turn away from the attack. So numb with cold was he, and so saddened by the sight of the caribou that he was too weak to hunt, that he simply knelt there helplessly, waiting for the wolf to spring.

He thought of his family and how he had failed them and left them to die alone, and he knew he would start to cry again. He fought back the sob that rose inside him, and through clenched teeth he whispered, "I will not show fear. I will not show this animal my fear. I will not die with my eyes frozen tight with tears."

Imitating his grandmother, he tipped back his head and let his cry of sadness turn into a long wolflike howl.

He waited, shivering with cold and fear, expecting to feel the fierce lunging weight of the wolf against him, the hot breath, the fur, the lean muscles, the fury of the slashing white teeth. But the attack did not come.

When Panniq dared to look again, he saw the huge blue wolf stand up and stretch itself lazily like a great thin husky dog. With a shock he saw another wolf stand up. It was the wolf's mate. She was long-legged and narrow-chested, lighter in color, with a thick, beautiful coat, black muzzle, ears held forward and alert, and big yellow eyes that seemed to stare straight through him. Tail down, she waited patiently for her mate to decide how they should take their prey.

Panniq could scarcely believe what he saw as the big male wolf turned and trotted past his mate, leading her carelessly away, across the plain toward the scattered herd. Heads up, they sniffed the air, testing the rich smell of caribou. As they chose their direction, they gathered speed and ran upwind.

When they reached a hollow in the ground where they could not be seen by the caribou, Panniq saw their run turn into a long, fast lope. They began to close in on the caribou as they crossed the snow ridge like two pale blue shadows in the moonlight. They moved now in a smooth, lunging rush, their wide padded paws hurling them across the snow until they were almost among the nearest of the unsuspecting animals.

When the caribou saw these two deadly enemies rushing in at them, they flung back their heads in fright and scattered in every direction, making the dry snow crystals fly from beneath their wide splayed hoofs. Then the caribou came together again into a loose herd, and stretching out their necks, they galloped across the snow, so beautifully and so swiftly that no wolf could catch them.

But these lean wolf mates were tireless, steady runners and wise, expert killers. Immediately they singled out a young male caribou that seemed fatter, perhaps, and slower than the rest. Soon this single fleeing caribou panicked and separated from the others. Quickly the wolves drove him away from the herd.

It was a familiar sight to Panniq, with the caribou running in the center and the two shadowlike creatures, one on either side, closely following their prey, imitating his every turn across the rolling snowdrifts of the plain. All three were tiring as they settled into a long, steady gait, moving more slowly, turning in a huge half circle. They were coming straight toward Panniq. The caribou, openmouthed and gasping for his life, left a light trail of vapor in the freezing air as the two wolves forced him up through the soft snow that had drifted along the edge of the ridge.

Panniq rose up onto his knees again, steadying himself with trembling hands, watching the chase like a hungry animal. He could hear the caribou snort and see its nostrils blown wide and its eyes rolled back in fear and strain.

When they were nearly upon him, Panniq saw the female wolf surge forward with a new burst of speed. For a moment she ran beside the fleeing animal like its own swift shadow. Then using her shoulder, she flung her weight against the shoulder of the running caribou, causing it to stumble and break its long, smooth stride.

That one faltering step was all the male wolf needed. As he swept in, he lunged at the prey, using his teeth, his powerful weight, and all his muscles to fling the caribou to the snow. In an instant the killing was done and the long, terrifying chase was ended.

Mouths open, tongues lolling, the two wolves stood above their prey, silently watching Panniq as he swayed before them. He tried desperately to keep his head up to watch them. He could scarcely believe what he saw. They ate not one bite of their kill, but stood staring at him, until the female gave a low whine and leaped across the fallen caribou, bumping her mate lightly with her shoulder as a signal. Together they trotted off and lay down beside each other some distance along the ridge to watch Panniq.

Slowly, painfully, he made his way down toward the caribou, stumbling twice as he went, but rising again and crawling, dragging himself over the hard-packed snow until at last he was able to lay his cheek against its warm, furry side. With his father's knife he slashed the caribou open and ate its hot red liver. Then he lay on his back and watched the stars.

It was not long until he felt the warmth and strength of life start to spread gently back into his bones. Hot fluid seemed to flow into his freezing muscles, gently easing their pain. The powerful idea that he might live again slowly came to him. He knew inside himself that his family who had saved their strength would still be alive.

Kneeling again and growing stronger, treasuring his new feeling of hope, he used the knife quickly and cleverly. He removed the caribou's thick, warm hide. Then with his knife and the soft heel of his boot, Panik broke the sharp crust of snow and hollowed out a soft nest below the level of the wind. Wrapping himself in the warm fur, he lay down and stared up at the bone-white face of the watching moon.

In the morning his strength would come back and he would take his father's bow and arrows and stalk the caribou. He would kill only as many as he had fingers on his hands, and he would carry back to their camp the finest one of these.

Panniq imagined he could faintly hear the drum as he proudly carried a young caribou into the camp. He heard himself shout to them joyfully, saying, "Look at me. Look at me. All the magic of your singing has not brought you food. But see, I have brought you food. I have brought you caribou meat, and much more lies frozen, ready for your feasting out there to the west."

Then he remembered that he was not alive because of his own cleverness, nor had this first meat come from the skill of his hunting. Life was not so simple as that. He thought of the fresh human tracks along the wolf run. He knew now that his grandfather and his grandmother had sent their spirits with the wolves to help him.

Panniq sat up in his shallow gravelike hole in the snow, still wrapped in the new caribou skin. He looked along the ridge at the two wolf shadows lying together, and he called out to them, saying, "Thank you, Grandfather. Thank you, Grandmother." At last he had been given the power to recognize them both. "Thank you for my life," he said.

And then he lay down and went to sleep.